THROUGH A GLASS, CLEARLY

Few writers need as little introduction as does Isaac Asimov: anyone at all acquainted with science-fiction must have read something he has written. Creator of the famous "Three Laws of Robotics"; author of novels like the "Foundation" trilogy; nearly 150 short stories; a general science column on a monthly basis in *The Magazine of Fantasy and Science Fiction* since November, 1958; the "Good Doctor", as he is affectionately known in the world of science-fiction, is a titan without peer.

The four stories in this book are collected in volume form for the first time and, as you would expect, are a combination of witty entertainment and brilliant scientific imagination. In a recent magazine article, the Good Doctor wrote: "I love being a writer; I have always loved being a writer." Thousands of readers hope that this love affair will never end.

TOM BOARDMAN, JR.

*Also by Isaac Asimov and available
in the NEL series*

SPACE RANGER
THE BIG SUN OF MERCURY
PIRATES OF THE ASTEROIDS

Through A Glass, Clearly

ISAAC ASIMOV

NEW ENGLISH LIBRARY
TIMES MIRROR

ACKNOWLEDGEMENTS

Breeds There A Man and *Belief*, copyright 1951 and 1953 by Street & Smith Publications, Inc., for *Astounding Science Fiction* (now *Analog Science Fiction—Science Fact*).

The C-Chute, copyright 1951 by Galaxy Publishing Corporation for *Galaxy Science Fiction*.

It's Such a Beautiful Day, copyright 1954 by Ballantine Books Inc., for *Star Science Fiction Stories, No. 3.*

NEL Books are published by
New English Library Limited, from Barnard's Inn, Holborn, London E.C.1.
Made and printed in Great Britqin by Hazell Watson & Vlney Ltd, Aylesbury, Bucks

450027155

Contents

IT'S SUCH A BEAUTIFUL DAY 7

BELIEF 28

BREEDS THERE A MAN...? 58

THE C-CHUTE 92

It's Such a Beautiful Day

On April 12, 2117, the field-modulator brake-valve in the Door belonging to Mrs. Richard Hanshaw depolarized for reasons unknown. As a result, Mrs. Hanshaw's day was completely upset and her son, Richard, Jr., first developed his strange neurosis.

It was the type of thing you would find listed as a neurosis in the usual textbooks and certainly young Richard behaved, in most respects, just as a well-brought-up twelve-year-old in prosperous circumstances ought to behave.

And yet from April 12 on, Richard Hanshaw, Jr., could only with regret ever persuade himself to go through a Door.

Of all this, on April 12, Mrs. Hanshaw had no premonition. She woke in the morning (an ordinary morning) as her mekkano slithered gently into the room, with a cup of coffee on a small tray. Mrs. Hanshaw was planning a visit to New York in the afternoon and she had several things to do first that could not quite be trusted to a mekkano, so after one or two sips, she stepped out of bed.

The mekkano backed away, moving silently along the diamagnetic field that kept its oblong body half an inch above the floor, and moved back to the kitchen, where its simple computer was quite adequate to set the proper controls on the various kitchen appliances in order that an appropriate breakfast might be prepared.

Mrs. Hanshaw, having bestowed the usual sentimental glance upon the cubograph of her dead husband, passed through the stages of her morning ritual with a certain contentment. She could hear her son across the hall clattering through his, but she knew she need not interfere with him. The mekkano was well adjusted to see to it, as a matter of course, that he was showered, that he had on a change of clothing, and that he would eat a nourishing breakfast. The tergo-shower she had had installed the year before made the morning wash and dry so quick and pleasant that, really, she felt certain Dickie would wash even without supervision.

7

On a morning like this, when she was busy, it would certainly not be necessary for her to do more than deposit a casual peck on the boy's cheek before he left. She heard the soft chime the mekkano sounded to indicate approaching school time and she floated down the force-lift to the lower floor (her hair-style for the day only sketchily designed, as yet) in order to perform that motherly duty.

She found Richard standing at the door, with his text-reels and pocket projector dangling by their strap and a frown on his face.

"Say, Mom," he said, looking up, "I dialed the school's co-ords but nothing happens."

She said, almost automatically, "Nonsense, Dickie. I never heard of such a thing."

"Well, you try."

Mrs. Hanshaw tried a number of times. Strange, the school door was always set for general reception. She tried other co-ordinates. Her friends' Doors might not be set for reception, but there would be a signal at least, and then she could explain.

But nothing happened at all. The Door remained an inactive gray barrier despite all her manipulations. It was obvious that the Door was out of order—and only five months after its annual fall inspection by the company.

She was quite angry about it.

It *would* happen on a day when she had much planned. She thought petulantly of the fact that a month earlier she had decided against installing a subsidiary Door on the ground that it was an unnecessary expense. How was she to know that Doors were getting to be so *shoddy?*

She stepped to the visiphone while the anger still burned in her and said to Richard, "You just go down the road, Dickie, and use the Williamsons' Door."

Ironically, in view of later developments, Richard balked. "Aw, gee, Mom, I'll get dirty. Can't I stay home till the Door is fixed?"

And, as ironically, Mrs. Hanshaw insisted. With her finger on the combination board of the phone, she said, "You won't get dirty if you put flexies on your shoes, and don't forget to brush yourself well before you go into their house."

"But, golly—"

"No back-talk, Dickie. You've got to be in school. Just let me see you walk out of here. And quickly, or you'll be late."

The mekkano, an advanced model and very responsive, was already standing before Richard with flexies in one appendage.

8

Richard pulled the transparent plastic shields over his shoes and moved down the hall with visible reluctance. "I don't even know how to work this thing, Mom."

"You just push that button," Mrs. Hanshaw called. "The red button. Where it says 'For emergency Use.' And don't dawdle. Do you want the mekkano to go along with you?"

"Gosh, no," he called back, morosely, "what do you think I am? A baby? Gosh!" His muttering was cut off by a slam.

With flying fingers, Mrs. Hanshaw punched the appropriate combination on the phone board and thought of the things she intended saying to the company about this.

Joe Bloom, a reasonably young man, who had gone through technology school with added training in force-field mechanics, was at the Hanshaw residence in less than half an hour. He was really quite competent, though Mrs. Hanshaw regarded his youth with deep suspicion.

She opened the movable house-panel when he first signaled and her sight of him was as he stood there, brushing at himself vigorously to remove the dust of the open air. He took off his flexies and dropped them where he stood. Mrs. Hanshaw closed the house-panel against the flash of raw sunlight that had entered. She found herself irrationally hoping that the step-by-step trip from the public Door had been an unpleasant one. Or perhaps that the public Door itself had been out of order and the youth had had to lug his tools even farther than the necessary two hundred yards. She wanted the Company, or its representative at least, to suffer a bit. It would teach them what broken Doors meant.

But he seemed cheerful and unperturbed as he said, "Good morning, ma'am. I came to see about your Door."

"I'm glad someone did," said Mrs. Hanshaw, ungraciously. "My day is quite ruined."

"Sorry, ma'am. What seems to be the trouble?"

"It just won't work. Nothing at all happens when you adjust co-ords," said Mrs. Hanshaw. "There was no warning at all. I had to send my son out to the neighbors through that—that thing."

She pointed to the entrance through which the repair man had come.

He smiled and spoke out of the conscious wisdom of his own specialized training in Doors. "That's a door, too, ma'am. You don't give that kind a capital letter when you write it. It's a hand-door, sort of. It used to be the only kind once."

9

"Well, at least it works. My boy's had to go out in the dirt and germs."

"It's not bad outside today, ma'am," he said, with the connoisseur-like air of one whose profession forced him into the open nearly every day. "Sometimes it *is* real unpleasant. But I guess you want I should fix this here Door, ma'am, so I'll get on with it."

He sat down on the floor, opened the large tool case he had brought with him and in half a minute, by use of a point-demagnetizer, he had the control panel removed and a set of intricate vitals exposed.

He whistled to himself as he placed the fine electrodes of the field-analyzer on numerous points, studying the shifting needles on the dials. Mrs. Hanshaw watched him, arms folded.

Finally, he said, "Well, here's something," and with a deft twist, he disengaged the brake valve.

He tapped it with a fingernail and said, "This here brake-valve is depolarized, ma'am. There's your whole trouble." He ran his finger along the little pigeonholes in his tool case and lifted out a duplicate of the object he had taken from the door mechanism. "These things just go all of a sudden. Can't predict it."

He put the control panel back and stood up. "It'll work now, ma'am."

He punched a reference combination, blanked it, then punched another. Each time, the dull gray of the Door gave way to a deep blackness. He said, "Will you sign here, ma'am? and put down your charge number, too, please? Thank you, ma'am."

He punched a new combination, that of his home factory, and with a polite touch of finger to forehead, he stepped through the Door. As his body entered the blackness, it cut off sharply. Less and less of him was visible and the tip of his tool case was the last thing that showed. A second after he had passed through completely, the Door turned back to dull gray.

Half an hour later, when Mrs. Hanshaw had finally completed her interrupted preparations and was fuming over the misfortune of the morning, the phone buzzed annoyingly and her real troubles began.

Miss Elizabeth Robbins was distressed. Little Dick Hanshaw had always been a good pupil. She hated to report him like this. And yet, she told herself, his actions were certainly queer. And she would talk to his mother, not to the principal.

She slipped out to the phone during the morning study period,

10

leaving a student in charge. She made her connection and found herself staring at Mrs. Hanshaw's handsome and somewhat formidable head.

Miss Robbins quailed, but it was too late to turn back. She said, diffidently, "Mrs. Hanshaw, I'm Miss Robbins." She ended on a rising note.

Mrs. Hanshaw looked blank, then said, "Richard's teacher?" That, too, ended on a rising note.

"That's right. I called you, Mrs. Hanshaw," Miss Robbins plunged right into it, "to tell you that Dick was quite late to school this morning."

"He *was?* But that couldn't be. I saw him leave."

Miss Robbins looked astonished. She said, "You mean you saw him use the Door?"

Mrs. Hanshaw said quickly, "Well, no. Our Door was temporarily out of order. I sent him to a neighbor and he used that Door."

"Are you sure?"

"Of course I'm sure. I wouldn't lie to you."

"No, no, Mrs. Hanshaw. I wasn't implying that at all. I meant are you sure he found the way to the neighbor? He might have got lost."

"Ridiculous. We have the proper maps, and I'm sure Richard knows the location of every house in District A-3." Then, with the quiet pride of one who knows what is her due, she added, "Not that he ever needs to know, of course. The co-ords are all that are necessary at any time."

Miss Robbins, who came from a family that had always had to economize rigidly on the use of its Doors (the price of power being what it was) and who had therefore run errands on foot until quite an advanced age, resented the pride. She said, quite clearly, "Well, I'm afraid, Mrs. Hanshaw, that Dick did not use the neighbor's Door. He was over an hour late to school and the condition of his flexies made it quite obvious that he tramped cross-country. They were *muddy.*"

"*Muddy?*" Mrs. Hanshaw repeated the emphasis on the word. "What did he say? What was his excuse?"

Miss Robbins couldn't help but feel a little glad at the discomfiture of the other woman. She said, "He wouldn't talk about it. Frankly, Mrs. Hanshaw, he seems ill. That's why I called you. Perhaps you might want to have a doctor look at him."

"Is he running a temperature?" The mother's voice went shrill.

"Oh, no. I don't mean physically ill. It's just his attitude and

11

the look in his eyes." She hesitated, then said with every attempt at delicacy, "I thought perhaps a routine checkup with a psychic probe—"

She didn't finish. Mrs. Hanshaw, in a chilled voice and with what was as close to a snort as her breeding would permit, said, "Are you implying that Richard is *neurotic?*"

"Oh, no, Mrs. Hanshaw, but—"

"It certainly sounded so. The idea! He has always been perfectly healthy. I'll take this up with him when he gets home. I'm sure there's a perfectly normal explanation which he'll give to *me.*"

The connection broke abruptly, and Miss Robbins felt hurt and uncommonly foolish. After all she had only tried to help, to fulfill what she considered an obligation to her students.

She hurried back to the classroom with a glance at the metal face of the wall clock. The study period was drawing to an end. English Composition next.

But her mind wasn't completely on English Composition. Automatically, she called the students to have them read selections from their literary creations. And occasionally she punched one of those selections on tape and ran it through the small vocalizer to show the students how English *should* be read.

The vocalizer's mechanical voice, as always, dripped perfection, but, again as always, lacked character. Sometimes, she wondered if it was wise to try to train the students into speech that was divorced from individuality and geared only to a mass-average accent and intonation.

Today, however, she had no thought for that. It was Richard Hanshaw she watched. He sat quietly in his seat, quite obviously indifferent to his surroundings. He was lost deep in himself and just not the same boy he had been. It was obvious to her that he had had some unusual experience that morning and, really, she was right to call his mother, although perhaps she ought not to have made the remark about the probe. Still it was quite the thing these days. All sorts of people got probed. There wasn't any disgrace attached to it. Or there shouldn't be, anyway.

She called on Richard, finally. She had to call twice, before he responded and rose to his feet.

The general subject assigned had been: "If you had your choice of travelling on some ancient vehicle, which would you choose, and why?" Miss Robbins tried to use the topic every semester. It was a good one because it carried a sense of history with it. It forced the youngster to think about the manner of living of people in past ages.

She listened while Richard read in a low voice.

"If I had my choice of ancient vehicles," he said, pronouncing the 'h' in vehicles, "I would choose the stratoliner. It travels slow like all vehicles but it is clean. Because it travels in the stratosphere, it must be all enclosed so that you are not likely to catch disease. You can see the stars if it is night time almost as good as in a planetarium. If you look down you can see the Earth like a map or maybe see clouds—" He went on for several hundred more words.

She said brightly when he had finished reading, "It's pronounced vee-ick-ulls, Richard. No 'h.' Accent on the first syllable. And you don't say 'travels slow' or 'see good.' What do you say, class?"

There was a small chorus of responses and she went on, "That's right. Now what is the difference between an adjective and an adverb? Who can tell me?"

And so it went on. Lunch passed. Some pupils stayed to eat; some went home. Richard stayed. Miss Robbins noted that, as usually he didn't.

The afternoon passed, too, and then there was the final bell and the usual upsurging hum as twenty-five boys and girls rattled their belongings together and took their leisurely place in the line.

Miss Robbins clapped her hands together. "Quickly, children. Come Zelda, take your place."

"I dropped my tape-punch, Miss Robbins," shrilled the girl, defensively.

"Well, pick it up, pick it up. Now children, be brisk, be brisk."

She pushed the button that slid a section of the wall into a recess and revealed the gray blankness of a large Door. It was not the usual Door that the occasional student used in going home for lunch, but an advanced model that was one of the prides of this well-to-do private school.

In addition to its double width, it possessed a large and impressively gear-filled "automatic serial finder" which was capable of adjusting the door for a number of different co-ordinates at automatic intervals.

At the beginning of the semester, Miss Robbins always had to spend an afternoon with the mechanic, adjusting the device for the co-ordinates of the homes of the new class. But then, thank goodness, it rarely needed attention for the remainder of the term.

The class lined up alphabetically, first girls, then boys. The door went velvety black and Hester Adams waved her hand and stepped through. "By-y-y—"

13

The 'bye was cut off in the middle, as it almost always was.

The door went gray, then black again, and Theresa Cantrocchi went through. Gray, black, Zelda Charlowicz. Gray, black, Patricia Coombs. Gray, black, Sara May Evans.

The line grew smaller as the Door swallowed them one by one, depositing each at her home. Of course, an occasional mother forgot to leave the house Door on special reception at the appropriate time and then the school Door remained gray. Automatically, after a minute-long wait, the Door went on to the next combination in line and the pupil in question had to wait till it was all over, after which a phone call to the forgetful parent would set things right. This was always bad for the pupils involved, especially the sensitive ones who took seriously the implication that they were little thought of at home. Miss Robbins always tried to impress this on visiting parents, but it happened at least once every semester just the same.

The girls were all through now. John Abramowitz stepped through and then Edwin Byrne—

Of course, another trouble, and a more frequent one was the boy or girl who got into line out of place. They *would* do it despite the teacher's sharpest watch, particularly at the beginning of the term when the proper order was less familiar to them.

When that happened, children would be popping into the wrong houses by the half-dozen and would have to be sent back. It always meant a mixup that took minutes to straighten out and parents were invariably irate.

Miss Robbins was suddenly aware that the line had stopped. She spoke sharply to the boy at the head of the line.

"Step through, Samuel. What are you waiting for?"

Samuel Jones raised a complacent countenance and said, "It's not my combination, Miss Robbins."

"Well, whose is it?" She looked impatiently down the line of five remaining boys. Who was out of place?

"It's Dick Hanshaw's, Miss Robbins."

"Where is he?"

Another boy answered, with the rather repulsive tone of self-righteousness all children automatically assume in reporting the deviations of their friends to elders in authority, "He went through the fire door, Miss Robbins."

"What?"

The schoolroom Door had passed on to another combination and Samuel Jones passed through. One by one, the rest followed.

Miss Robbins was alone in the classroom. She stepped to the

14

fire door. It was a small affair, manually operated, and hidden behind a bend in the wall so that it would not break up the uniform structure of the room.

She opened it a crack. It was there as a means of escape from the building in case of fire, a device which was enforced by an anachronistic law that did not take into account the modern methods of automatic fire-fighting that all public buildings used. There was nothing outside, but the—outside. The sunlight was harsh and a dusty wind was blowing.

Miss Robbins closed the door. She was glad she had called Mrs. Hanshaw. She had done her duty. More than ever, it was obvious that something was wrong with Richard. She suppressed the impulse to phone again.

Mrs. Hanshaw did not go to New York that day. She remained home in a mixture of anxiety and an irrational anger, the latter directed against the impudent Miss Robbins.

Some fifteen minutes before school's end, her anxiety drove her to the Door. Last year she had had it equipped with an automatic device which activated it to the school's co-ordinates at five of three and kept it so, barring manual adjustment, until Richard arrived.

Her eyes were fixed on the Door's dismal gray (why couldn't an inactive force-field be any other color, something more lively and cheerful?) and waited. Her hands felt cold as she squeezed them together.

The Door turned black at the precise second but nothing happened. The minutes passed and Richard was late. Then quite late. Then very late.

It was a quarter of four and she was distracted. Normally, she would have phoned the school, but she couldn't, she couldn't. Not after that teacher had deliberately cast doubts on Richard's mental well-being. How could she?

Mrs. Hanshaw moved about restlessly, lighting a cigarette with fumbling fingers, then smudging it out. Could it be something quite normal? Could Richard be staying after school for some reason? Surely he would have told her in advance. A gleam of light struck her; he knew she was planning to go to New York and might not be back till late in the evening—

No, he would surely have told her. Why fool herself?

Her pride was breaking. She would have to call the school, or even (she closed her eyes and teardrops squeezed through between the lashes) the police.

And when she opened her eyes, Richard stood before her, eyes on the ground and his whole bearing that of someone waiting for a blow to fall.

"Hello, Mom."

Mrs. Hanshaw's anxiety transmuted itself instantly (in a manner known only to mothers) into anger. "Where have you been, Richard?"

And then, before she could go further into the refrain concerning careless, unthinking sons and broken-hearted mothers, she took note of his appearance in greater detail, and gasped in utter horror.

She said, "You've been in the open."

Her son looked down at his dusty shoes (minus flexies), at the dirt marks that streaked his lower arms and at the small, but definite tear in his shirt. He said, "Gosh, Mom, I just thought I'd—" and he faded out.

She said, "Was there anything wrong with the school Door?"

"No, Mom."

"Do you realize I've been worried sick about you?" She waited vainly for an answer. "Well, I'll talk to you afterward, young man. First, you're taking a bath, and every stitch of your clothing is being thrown out. Mekkano!"

But the mekkano had already reacted properly to the phrase "taking a bath" and was off to the bathroom in its silent glide.

"You take your shoes off right here," said Mrs. Hanshaw, "then march after mekkano."

Richard did as he was told with a resignation that placed him beyond futile protest.

Mrs. Hanshaw picked up the soiled shoes between thumb and forefinger and dropped them down the disposal chute which hummed in faint dismay at the unexpected load. She dusted her hands carefully on a tissue which she allowed to float down the chute after the shoes.

She did not join Richard at dinner but let him eat in the worse-than-lack-of-company of the mekkano. This, she thought, would be an active sign of her displeasure and would do more than any amount of scolding or punishment to make him realize that he had done wrong. Richard, she frequently told herself, was a sensitive boy.

But she went up to see him at bedtime.

She smiled at him and spoke softly. She thought that would be the best way. After all, he had been punished already.

She said, "What happened today, Dickie-boy?" She had called

16

him that when he was a baby and just the sound of the name softened her nearly to tears.

But he only looked away and his voice was stubborn and cold. "I just don't like going through those darn Doors, Mom."

"But why ever not?"

He shuffled his hands over the filmy sheet (fresh, clean, antiseptic and, of course, disposable after each use) and said, "I just don't like them."

"But then how do you expect to go to school, Dickie?"

"I'll get up early," he mumbled.

"But there's nothing wrong with Doors."

"Don't like 'em." He never once looked at her.

She said, despairingly. "Oh, well, you have a good sleep and tomorrow morning you'll feel much better."

She kissed him and left the room, automatically passing her hand through the photo-cell beam and in that manner dimming the room lights.

But she had trouble sleeping herself that night. Why should Dickie dislike Doors so suddenly? They had never bothered him before. To be sure, the Door had broken down in the morning but that should make him appreciate them all the more.

Dickie was behaving so unreasonably.

Unreasonably? That reminded her of Miss Robbins and her diagnosis and Mrs. Hanshaw's soft jaw set in the darkness and privacy of her bedroom. Nonsense! The boy was upset and a night's sleep was all the therapy he needed.

But the next morning when she arose, her son was not in the house. The mekkano could not speak but it could answer questions with gestures of its appendages equivalent to a yes or no, and it did not take Mrs. Hanshaw more than half a minute to ascertain that the boy had arisen thirty minutes earlier than usual, skimped his shower, and darted out of the house.

But not by way of the Door.

Out the other way—through the door. Small "d".

Mrs. Hanshaw's visiphone signaled genteelly at 3:10 P.M. that day. Mrs. Hanshaw guessed the caller and having activated the receiver, saw that she had guessed correctly. A quick glance in the mirror to see that she was properly calm after a day of abstracted concern and worry and then she keyed in her own transmission.

"Yes, Miss Robbins," she said coldly.

Richard's teacher was a bit breathless. She said, "Mrs. Hanshaw, Richard has deliberately left through the fire door although

I told him to use the regular Door. I do not know where he went."

Mrs. Hanshaw said, carefully, "He left to come home."

Miss Robbins looked dismayed, "Do you approve of this?"

Pale-faced, Mrs. Hanshaw set about putting the teacher in her place. "I don't think it is up to you to criticize. If my son does not choose to use the Door, it is his affair and mine. I don't think there is any school ruling that would force him to use the Door, is there?" Her bearing quite plainly intimated that if there were she would see to it that it was changed.

Miss Robbins flushed and had time for one quick remark before contact was broken. She said, "I'd have him probed. I really would."

Mrs. Hanshaw remained standing before the quartzinium plate, staring blindly at its blank face. Her sense of family placed her for a few moments quite firmly on Richard's side. Why *did* he have to use the Door if he chose not to? And then she settled down to wait and pride battled the gnawing anxiety that something after all was wrong with Richard.

He came home with a look of defiance on his face, but his mother, with a strenuous effort at self-control, met him as though nothing were out of the ordinary.

For weeks, she followed that policy. It's nothing, she told herself. It's a vagary. He'll grow out of it.

It grew into an almost normal state of affairs. Then, too, every once in a while, perhaps three days in a row, she would come down to breakfast to find Richard waiting sullenly at the Door, then using it when school time came. She always refrained from commenting on the matter.

Always, when he did that, and especially when he followed it up by arriving home via the Door, her heart grew warm and she thought, "Well, it's over." But always with the passing of one day, two or three, he would return like an addict to his drug and drift silently out by the door—small "d"—before she woke.

And each time she thought despairingly of psychiatrists and probes, and each time the vision of Miss Robbins' low-bred satisfaction at (possibly) learning of it, stopped her, although she was scarcely aware that that was the true motive.

Meanwhile she lived with it and made the best of it. The mekkano was instructed to wait at the door—small "d"—with a Tergo kit and a change of clothing. Richard washed and changed without resistance. His underthings, socks and flexies were disposable in any case, and Mrs. Hanshaw bore uncomplainingly the expense of daily disposal of shirts. Trousers she finally allowed to go a week before disposal on condition of rigorous nightly cleansing.

One day she suggested that Richard accompany her on a trip to New York. It was more a vague desire to keep him in sight than part of any purposeful plan. He did not object. He was even happy. He stepped right through the Door, unconcerned. He didn't hesitate. He even lacked the look of resentment he wore on those mornings he used the Door to go to school.

Mrs. Hanshaw rejoiced. This could be a way of weaning him back into Door usage, and she racked her ingenuity for excuses to make trips with Richard. She even raised her power bill to quite unheard-off heights by suggesting, and going through with, a trip to Canton for the day in order to witness a Chinese festival.

That was on a Sunday, and the next morning Richard marched directly to the hole in the wall he always used. Mrs. Hanshaw, having wakened particularly early, witnessed that. For once, badgered past endurance, she called after him plaintively, "Why not the Door, Dickie?"

He said, briefly, "It's all right for Canton," and stepped out of the house.

So that plan ended in failure. And then, one day, Richard came home soaking wet. The mekkano hovered about him uncertainly and Mrs. Hanshaw just returned from a four-hour visit with her sister in Iowa, cried, "Richard Hanshaw!"

He said, hang-dog fashion, "It started raining. All of a sudden, it started raining."

For a moment, the word didn't register with her. Her own school days and her studies of geography were twenty years in the past. And then she remembered and caught the vision of water pouring recklessly and endlessly down from the sky—a mad cascade of water with no tap to turn off, no button to push, and no contact to break.

She said, "And you stayed out in it?"

He said, "Well, gee, Mom, I came home fast as I could. I didn't know it was going to rain."

Mrs. Hanshaw had nothing to say. She was appalled and the sensation filled her too full for words to find a place.

Two days later, Richard found himself with a running nose, and a dry, scratchy throat. Mrs. Hanshaw had to admit that the virus of disease had found a lodging in her house, as though it were a miserable hovel of the Iron age.

It was over this that her stubbornness and pride broke and she

19

admitted to herself that, after all, Richard had to have psychiatric help.

Mrs. Hanshaw chose a psychiatrist with care. Her first impulse was to find one at a distance. For a while, she considered stepping directly into San Francisco Medical Center and choosing one at random.

And then it occurred to her that by doing that she would become merely an anonymous consultant. She would have no way of obtaining any greater consideration for herself than would be forthcoming to any public-Door user of the city slums. Now if she remained in her own community, her word would carry weight—

She consulted the district map. It was one of that excellent series prepared by Doors, Inc., and distributed free of charge to their clients. Mrs. Hanshaw couldn't quite suppress that little thrill of civic pride as she unfolded the map. It wasn't a fine-print directory of Door co-ordinates only. It was an actual map, with each house carefully located.

And why not? District A-3 was a name of moment in the world, a badge of aristocracy. It was the first community on the planet to have been established on a completely Doored basis. The first, the largest, the wealthiest, the best-known. It needed no factories, no stores. It didn't even need roads. Each house was a little secluded castle, the Door of which had entry anywhere the world over where other Doors existed.

Carefully, she followed down the keyed listing of the five thousand families of District A-3. She knew it included several psychiatrists. The learned professions were well represented in A-3.

Doctor Hamilton Sloane was the second name she arrived at and her finger lingered upon the map. His office was scarcely two miles from the Hanshaw residence. She liked his name. The fact that he lived in A-3 was evidence of worth. And he was a neighbor, practically a neighbor. He would understand that it was a matter of urgency—and confidential.

Firmly, she put in a call to his office to make an appointment.

Doctor Hamilton Sloane was a comparatively young man, not quite forty. He was of good family and he had indeed heard of Mrs. Hanshaw.

He listened to her quietly and then said, "And this all began with the Door breakdown."

"That's right, doctor."

"Does he show any fear of the Doors?"

"Of course not. What an idea!" She was plainly startled.

"It's possible, Mrs. Hanshaw, it's possible. After all, when you stop to think of how a Door works it is rather a frightening thing, really. You step into a Door, and for an instant your atoms are converted into field-energies, transmitted to another part of space and reconverted into matter. For that instant you're not alive."

"I'm sure no one thinks of such things."

"But your son may. He witnessed the breakdown of the Door. He may be saying to himself, "What if the Door breaks down just as I'm half-way through?""

"But that's nonsense. He still uses the Door. He's even been to Canton with me; Canton, China. And as I told you, he uses it for school about once or twice a week."

"Freely? Cheerfully?"

"Well," said Mrs. Hanshaw, reluctantly, "he does seem a bit put out by it. But, really Doctor, there isn't much use talking about it, is there? If you would do a quick probe, see where the trouble was," and she finished on a bright note, "why, that would be all. I'm sure it's quite a minor thing."

Dr. Sloane sighed. He detested the word "probe" and there was scarcely any word he heard oftener.

"Mrs. Hanshaw," he said patiently, "there is no such thing as a quick probe. Now I know the mag-strips are full of it and it's a rage in some circles, but it's much overrated."

"Are you serious?"

"Quite. The probe is very complicated and the theory is that it traces mental circuits. You see, the cells of the brains are interconnected in a large variety of ways. Some of those interconnected paths are more used than others. They represent habits of thought, both conscious and unconscious. Theory has it that these paths in any given brain can be used to diagnose mental ills early and with certainty."

"Well, then?"

"But subjection to the probe is quite a fearful thing, especially to a child. It's a traumatic experience. It takes over an hour. And even then, the results must be sent to the Central Psychoanalytical Bureau for analysis, and that could take weeks. And on top of that, Mrs. Hanshaw, there are many psychiatrists who think the theory of probe-analyses to be most uncertain."

Mrs. Hanshaw compressed her lips. "You mean nothing can be done."

Dr. Sloane smiled. "Not at all. There were psychiatrists for centuries before there were probes. I suggest that you let me talk to the boy."

"Talk to him? Is that all?"

"I'll come to you for background information when necessary, but the essential thing, I think, is to talk to the boy."

"Really, Dr. Sloane, I doubt if he'll discuss the matter with you. He won't talk to me about it and I'm his mother."

"That often happens," the psychiatrist assured her. "A child will sometimes talk more readily to a stranger. In any case, I cannot take the case otherwise."

Mrs. Hanshaw rose, not at all pleased. "When can you come, Doctor?"

"What about this coming Saturday? The boy won't be in school. Will you be busy?"

"We will be ready."

She made a dignified exit. Dr. Sloane accompanied her through the small reception room to his office Door and waited while she punched the co-ordinates of her house. He watched her pass through. She became a half-woman, a quarter-woman, an isolated elbow and foot, a nothing.

It *was* frightening.

Did a Door ever break down during passage, leaving half a body here and half there? He had never heard of such a case, but he imagined it could happen.

He returned to his desk and looked up the time of his next appointment. It was obvious to him that Mrs. Hanshaw was annoyed and disappointed at not having arranged for a psychic probe treatment.

Why, for God's sake? Why should a thing like the probe, an obvious piece of quackery in his own opinion, get such a hold on the general public? It must be part of this general trend towards machines. Anything man can do, machines can do better. Machines! More machines! Machines for anything and everything! O tempora! O mores!

Oh, hell!

His resentment of the probe was beginning to bother him. Was it a fear of technological unemployment, a basic insecurity on his part, a mechanophobia, if that was the word—

He made a mental note to discuss this with his own analyst.

Dr. Sloane had to feel his way. The boy wasn't a patient who had come to him, more or less anxious to talk, more or less anxious to be helped.

22

Under the circumstances it would have been best to keep his first meeting with Richard short and noncommittal. It would have been sufficient merely to establish himself as something less than a total stranger. The next time he would be someone Richard had seen before. The time after he would be an acquaintance, and after that a friend of the family.

Unfortunately, Mrs. Hanshaw was not likely to accept a long-drawn-out process. She would go searching for a probe and, of course, she would find it.

And harm the boy. He was certain of that.

It was for that reason he felt he must sacrifice a little of the proper caution and risk a small crisis.

An uncomfortable ten minutes had passed when he decided he must try. Mrs. Hanshaw was smiling in a rather rigid way, eyeing him narrowly, as though she expected verbal magic from him. Richard wriggled in his seat, unresponsive to Dr. Sloane's tentative comments, overcome with boredom and unable not to show it.

Dr. Sloane said, with casual suddenness, "Would you like to take a walk with me, Richard?"

The boy's eyes widened and he stopped wriggling. He looked directly at Dr. Sloane. "A walk, sir?"

"I mean, outside."

"Do you go—outside?"

"Sometimes. When I feel like it."

Richard was on his feet, holding down a squirming eagerness. "I didn't think anyone did."

"I do. And I like company."

The boy sat down, uncertainly. "Mom?—"

Mrs. Hanshaw had stiffened in her seat, her compressed lips radiating horror, but she managed to say, "Why certainly, Dickie. But watch yourself."

And she managed a quick and baleful glare at Dr. Sloane.

In one respect, Dr. Sloane had lied. He did *not* go outside "sometimes." He hadn't been in the open since early college days. True, he had been athletically inclined (still was to some extent) but in his time the indoor ultraviolet chambers, swimming pools and tennis courts had flourished. For those with the price, they were much more satisfactory than the outdoor equivalents, open to the elements as they were, could possibly be. There was no occasion to go outside.

So there was a crawling sensation about his skin when he felt wind touch it, and he put down his flexied shoes on bare grass with a gingerly movement.

"Hey, look at that." Richard was quite different now, laughing, his reserve broken down.

Dr. Sloane had time only to catch a flash of blue that ended in a tree. Leaves rustled and he lost it.

"What was it?"

"A bird," said Richard. "A blue kind of bird."

Dr. Sloane looked about him in amazement. The Hanshaw residence was on a rise of ground, and he could see for miles. The area was only lightly wooded and between clumps of trees, grass gleamed brightly in the sunlight.

Colors set in deeper green made red and yellow patterns. They were flowers. From the books he had viewed in the course of his lifetime and from the old video shows, he had learned enough so that all this had an eerie sort of familiarity.

And yet the grass was so trim, the flowers so patterned. Dimly, he realized he had been expecting something wilder. He said, "Who takes care of all this?"

Richard shrugged. "I dunno. Maybe the Mekkanos do it."

"Mekkanos?"

"There's loads of them around. Sometimes they got a sort of atomic knife they hold near the ground. It cuts the grass. And they're always fooling around with the flowers and things. There's one of them over there."

It was a small object, half a mile away. Its metal skin cast back highlights as it moved slowly over the gleaming meadow, engaged in some sort of activity that Dr. Sloane could not identify.

Dr. Sloane was astonished. Here it was a perverse sort of estheticism, a kind of conspicuous consumption—

"What's that?" he asked suddenly.

Richard looked. He said, "That's a house. Belongs to the Froehlichs. Co-ordinates, A-3, 23, 461. That little pointy building over there is the public Door."

Dr. Sloane was staring at the house. Was that what it looked like from the outside? Somehow he had imagined something much more cubic, and taller.

"Come along," shouted Richard, running ahead.

Dr. Sloane followed more sedately. "Do you know all the houses about here?"

"Just about."

"Where is A-23, 26, 475?" It was his own house, of course.

24

Richard looked about. "Let's see. Oh, sure, I know where it is—you see that water there?"

"Water?" Dr. Sloane made out a line of silver curving across the green.

"Sure. Real water. Just sort of running over rocks and things. It keeps running all the time. You can get across it if you step on the rocks. It's called a river."

More like a creek, thought Dr. Sloane. He had studied geography, of course, but what passed for the subject these days was really economic and cultural geography. Physical geography was almost an extinct science except among specialists. Still, he knew what rivers and creeks were, in a theoretical sort of way.

Richard was still talking. "Well, just past the river, over that hill with the big clump of trees and down the other side a way is A-23, 26, 475. It's a light green house with a white roof."

"It is?" Dr. Sloane was genuinely astonished. He hadn't known it was green.

Some small animal disturbed the grass in its anxiety to avoid the oncoming feet. Richard looked after it and shrugged. "You can't catch them. I tried."

A butterfly flitted past, a wavering bit of yellow. Dr. Sloane's eyes followed it.

There was a low hum that lay over the fields, interspersed with an occasional harsh, calling sound, a rattle, a twittering, a chatter that rose, then fell. As his ear accustomed itself to listening, Dr. Sloane heard a thousand sounds, and none were man-made.

A shadow fell upon the scene, advancing toward him, covering him. It was suddenly cooler and he looked upwards, startled.

Richard said, "It's just a cloud. It'll go away in a minute—looka these flowers. They're the kind that smell."

They were several hundred yards from the Hanshaw residence. The cloud passed and the sun shone once more. Dr. Sloane looked back and was appalled at the distance they had covered. If they moved out of sight of the house and if Richard ran off, would he be able to find his way back?

He pushed the thought away impatiently and looked out toward the line of water (nearer now) and past it to where his own house must be. He thought wonderingly: Light green?

He said, "You must be quite an explorer."

Richard said, with a shy pride, "When I go to school and come back, I always try to use a different route and see new things."

"But you don't go outside every morning, do you? Sometimes you use the Doors, I imagine."

"Oh, sure."

"Why is that, Richard?" Somehow, Dr. Sloane felt there might be significance in that point.

But Richard quashed him. With his eyebrows up and a look of astonishment on his face, he said, "Well, gosh, some mornings it rains and I *have* to use the Door. I hate that, but what can you do? About two weeks ago, I got caught in the rain and I—" he looked about him automatically, and his voice sank to a whisper "—caught a cold and wasn't Mom upset, though."

Dr. Sloane sighed. "Shall we go back now?"

There was a quick disappointment on Richard's face. "Aw, what for?"

"You remind me that your mother must be waiting for us."

"I guess so." The boy turned reluctantly.

They walked slowly back. Richard was saying, chattily, "I wrote a composition at school once about how if I could go on some ancient vehicle" (he pronounced it with exaggerated care) "I'd go in a stratoliner and look at stars and clouds and things. Oh, boy, I was sure nuts."

"You'd pick something else now?"

"You bet. I'd go in an aut'm'bile, real slow. Then I'd see everything there was."

Mrs. Hanshaw seemed troubled, uncertain. "You don't think it's abnormal, then, doctor?"

"Unusual, perhaps, but not abnormal. He likes the outside."

"But how can he? It's so dirty, so unpleasant."

"That's a matter of individual taste. A hundred years ago our ancestors were all outside most of the time. Even today, I dare say there are a million Africans who have never seen a Door."

"But Richard's always been taught to behave himself the way a decent person in District A-3 is supposed to behave," said Mrs. Hanshaw, fiercely. "Not like an African or—or an ancestor."

"That may be part of the trouble, Mrs. Hanshaw. He feels this urge to go outside and yet he feels it to be wrong. He's ashamed to talk about it to you or to his teacher. It forces him into sullen retreat and it could eventually be dangerous."

"Then how can we persuade him to stop?"

Dr. Sloane said, "Don't try. Channel the activity instead. The day your Door broke down, he was forced outside, found he liked it, and that set a pattern. He used the trip to school and back as an excuse to repeat that first exciting experience. Now suppose you agree to let him out of the house for two hours on Saturdays

26

and Sundays. Suppose he gets it through his head that after all he can go outside without necessarily having to go anywhere in the process. Don't you think he'll be willing to use the Door to go to school and back thereafter? And don't you think that will stop the trouble he's now having with his teacher and probably with his fellow-pupils?"

"But then will matters remain so? Must they? Won't he ever be normal again?"

Dr. Sloane rose to his feet. "Mrs. Hanshaw, he's as normal as need be right now. Right now, he's tasting the joys of the forbidden. If you co-operate with him, show that you don't disapprove, it will lose some of the attraction right there. Then, as he grows older, he will become more aware of the expectations and demands of society. He will learn to conform. After all, there is a little of the rebel in all of us, but it generally dies down as we grow old and tired. Unless, that is, it is unreasonably suppressed and allowed to build up pressure. Don't do that. Richard will be all right."

He walked to the Door.

Mrs. Hanshaw said, "And you don't think a probe will be necessary, doctor?"

He turned and said vehemently, "No, definitely not! There is nothing about the boy that requires it. Understand? Nothing!"

His fingers hesitated an inch from the combination board and the expression on his face grew lowering.

"What's the matter, Dr. Sloane?" asked Mrs. Hanshaw.

But he didn't hear her because he was thinking of the Door and the psychic probe and all the rising, choking tide of machinery. There is a little of the rebel in all of us, he thought.

So he said in a soft voice, as his hand fell away from the board and his feet turned away from the Door, "You know, it's such a beautiful day that I think I'll walk."

BELIEF

"Did you ever dream you were flying?" asked Dr. Roger Toomey of his wife.

Jane Toomey looked up. "Certainly!"

Her quick fingers didn't stop their nimble manipulations of the yarn out of which an intricate and quite useless doily was being created. The television set made a muted murmur in the room and the posturings on its screen were, out of long custom, disregarded.

Roger said, "Everyone dreams of flying at some time or other. It's universal. I've done it many times. That's what worries me."

Jane said, "I don't know what you're getting at, dear. I hate to say so." She counted stitches in an undertone.

"When you think about it, it makes you wonder. It's not really flying that you dream of. You have no wings; at least I never had any. There's no effort involved. You're just floating. That's it. Floating."

"When I fly," said Jane, "I don't remember any of the details. Except once I landed on top of City Hall and hadn't any clothes on. Somehow, no one ever seems to pay any attention to you when you're dream-nude. Ever notice that? You're dying of embarrassment but people just pass by."

She pulled at the yarn and the ball tumbled out of the bag and half across the floor. She paid no attention.

Roger shook his head slowly. At the moment, his face was pale and absorbed in doubt. It seemed all angles with its high cheekbones, its long straight nose and the widow's-peak hairline that was growing more pronounced with the years. He was thirty-five.

He said, "Have you ever wondered what makes you dream you're floating?"

"No, I haven't."

Jane Toomey was blond and small. Her prettiness was the fragile kind that does not impose itself upon you but rather creeps on you unaware. She had the bright blue eyes and pink cheeks of a porcelain doll. She was thirty.

Roger said, "Many dreams are only the mind's interpretation

28

of a stimulus imperfectly understood. The stimuli are forced into a reasonable context in a split second."

Jane said, "What are you talking about, darling?"

Roger said, "Look, I once dreamed I was in a hotel, attending a Physics convention. I was with old friends. Everything seemed quite normal. Suddenly, there was a confusion of shouting and for no reason at all I grew panicky. I ran to the door but it wouldn't open. One by one, my friends disappeared. They had no trouble leaving the room, but I couldn't see how they managed it. I shouted at them and they ignored me.

"It was borne in upon me that the hotel was on fire. I didn't smell smoke. I just knew there was a fire. I ran to the window and I could see a fire escape on the outside of the building. I ran to each window in turn but none led to the fire escape. I was quite alone in the room now. I leaned out the window, calling desperately. No one heard me.

"Then the fire engines were coming, little red smears darting along the streets. I remember that clearly. The alarm bells clanged sharply to clear traffic. I could hear them, louder and louder till the sound was splitting my skull. I awoke and, of course, the alarm clock was ringing.

"Now I can't have dreamed a long dream designed to arrive at the moment of the alarm-clock ring in a way that builds the alarm neatly into the fabric of the dream. It's much more reasonable to suppose that the dream began at the moment the alarm began and crammed all its sensation of duration into one split second. It was just a hurry-up device of my brain to explain this sudden noise that penetrated the silence."

Jane was frowning now. She put down her crocheting. "Roger! you've been behaving queerly since you got back from the College. You didn't eat much and now this ridiculous conversation. I've never heard you so morbid. What you need is a dose of bicarbonate."

"I need a little more than that," said Roger in a low voice. "Now what starts a floating dream?"

"If you don't mind, let's change the subject."

She rose, and with firm fingers turned up the sound on the television set. A young gentleman with hollow cheeks and a soulful tenor suddenly raised his voice and assured her, dulcetly, of his never ending love.

Roger turned it down again and stood with his back to the instrument.

"Levitation!" he said. "That's it. There is some way in which human beings can make themselves float. They have the capacity for it. It's just that they don't know how to use that capacity,—except when they sleep. Then, sometimes, they lift up just a little bit, a tenth of an inch maybe. It wouldn't be enough for anyone to notice even if they were watching, but it would be enough to deliver the proper sensation for the start of a floating dream."

"Roger, you're delirious. I wish you'd stop. Honestly."

He drove on. "Sometimes we sink down slowly and the sensation is gone. Then again, sometimes the float-control ends suddenly and we drop. Jane did you ever dream you were falling?"

"Yes, of c—"

"You're hanging on the side of a building or you're sitting at the edge of a seat and suddenly you're tumbling. There's the awful shock of falling and you snap awake, your breath gasping, your heart palpitating. You *did* fall. There's no other explanation."

Jane's expression, having passed slowly from bewilderment to concern, dissolved suddenly into sheepish amusement.

"Roger, you *devil*. And you fooled me! Oh, you rat!"

"What?"

"Oh, no. You can't play it out anymore. I know exactly what you're doing. You're making up a plot to a story and you're trying it out on me. I should know better than to listen to you."

Roger looked startled, even a little confused. He strode to her chair and looked down at her, "No, Jane."

"I don't see why not. You've been talking about writing fiction as long as I've known you. If you've got a plot, you might as well write it down. No use just frightening me with it." Her fingers flew as her spirits rose.

"Jane this is no story."

"But what else—"

"When I woke up this morning, *I dropped to the mattress!*"

He stared at her without blinking. "I dreamed that I was flying," he said. "It was clear and distinct. I remember every minute of it. I was lying on my back when I woke up. I was feeling comfortable and quite happy. I just wondered a little why the ceiling looked so queer. I yawned and stretched and *touched* the ceiling. For a minute, I just stared at my arm reaching upward and ending hard against the ceiling.

"Then I turned over. I didn't move a muscle, Jane. I just turned all in one piece because I wanted to. There I was, five feet above the bed. There you were on the bed, sleeping. I was frightened. I didn't know how to get down, but the minute I thought of getting

30

down, I dropped. I dropped slowly. The whole process was under perfect control.

"I stayed in bed fifteen minutes before I dared move. Then I got up, washed, dressed, and went to work."

Jane forced a laugh, "Darling, you had *better* write it up. But that's all right. You've just been working too hard."

"Please! Don't be banal."

"People work too hard, even though to say so is banal. After all, you were just dreaming fifteen minutes longer than you thought you were."

"It wasn't a dream."

"Of course it was. I can't even count the times I've dreamed I awoke and dressed and made breakfast; then really woke up and found it was all to do over again. I've even dreamed I was dreaming if you see what I mean. It can be awfully confusing."

"Look, Jane. I've come to you with a problem because you're the only one I feel I can come to. Please take me seriously."

Jane's blue eyes opened wide. "Darling! I'm taking you as seriously as I can. You're the Physics professor, not I. Gravitation is what you know about, not I. Would *you* take it seriously if I told you *I* had found myself floating?"

"No. *No!* That's the hell of it. I don't want to believe it, only I've got to. It was no dream, Jane. I tried to tell myself it was. You have no idea how I talked myself into that. By the time I got to class, I was sure it was a dream. You didn't notice anything queer about me at breakfast, did you?"

"Yes, I did, now that I think about it."

"Well, it wasn't very queer or you would have mentioned it. Anyway, I gave my nine o'clock lecture perfectly. By eleven, I had forgotten the whole incident. Then, just after lunch, I needed a book. I needed Page and—Well, the book doesn't matter; I just needed it. It was on an upper shelf, but I could reach it. Jane—"

He stopped.

"Well, go on. Roger."

"Look, did you ever try to pick up something that's just a step away? You bend and automatically take a step toward it as you reach. It's completely involuntary. It's just your body's over-all co-ordination."

"All right. What of it?"

"I reached for the book and automatically took a step upward. On air, Jane! On empty air!"

"I'm going to call Jim Sarle, Roger."

"I'm not sick, damn it."

"I think he ought to talk to you. He's a friend. It won't be a doctor's visit. He'll just talk to you."

"And what good will that do?" Roger's face turned red with sudden anger.

"We'll see. Now sit down, Roger. Please." She walked to the phone.

He cut her off, seizing her wrist. "You don't believe me."

"Oh, Roger."

"You don't."

"I believe you. Of course, I believe you. I just want—"

"Yes. You just want Jim Sarle to talk to me. That's how much you believe me. I'm telling the truth but you want me to talk to a psychiatrist. Look, you don't have to take my word for anything. I can prove this. I can prove I can float."

"I *believe* you."

"Don't be a fool. I know when I'm being humored. Stand still! Now watch me."

He backed away to the middle of the room and without preliminary lifted off the floor. He *dangled;* with the toes of his shoes six empty inches from the carpet.

Jane's eyes and mouth were three round O's. She whispered, "Come down, Roger. Oh, dear heaven, come down."

He drifted down, his feet touching the floor without a sound. "You see?"

"Oh, my. Oh, my."

She stared at him, half-frightened, half-sick.

On the television set, a chesty female sang mutedly that flying high with some guy in the sky was her idea of nothing at all.

Roger Toomey stared into the bedroom's darkness. He whispered, "Jane."

"What?"

"You're not sleeping?"

"No."

"I can't sleep, either. I keep holding the headboard to make sure I'm . . . you know."

His hand moved restlessly and touched her face. She flinched, jerking away as though he carried an electric charge.

She said, "I'm sorry. I'm a little nervous."

"That's all right. I'm getting out of bed anyway."

"What are you going to do? You've got to sleep."

"Well, I can't, so there's no sense keeping you awake, too."

"Maybe nothing will happen. It doesn't have to happen every night. It didn't happen before last night."

"How do I know? Maybe I just never went up so high. Maybe I just never woke up and caught myself. Anyway, now it's different."

He was sitting up in bed, his legs bent, his arms clasping his knees, his forehead resting on them. He pushed the sheet to one side and rubbed his cheek against the soft flannel of his pyjamas.

He said, "It's bound to be different now. My mind's full of it. Once I'm asleep, once I'm not holding myself down consciously, why, up I'll go."

"I don't see why. It must be such an effort."

"That's the point. It isn't."

"But you're fighting gravity, aren't you?"

"I know, but there's still no effort. Look Jane, if I only *could* understand it, I wouldn't mind so much."

He dangled his feet out of bed and stood up. "I don't want to talk about it."

His wife muttered, "I don't want to, either." She started crying, fighting back the sobs and turning them into strangled moans, which sounded much worse.

Roger said, "I'm sorry, Jane. I'm getting you all wrought-up."

"No, don't touch me. Just . . . just leave me alone."

He took a few uncertain steps away from the bed.

She said, "Where are you going?"

"To the studio couch. Will you help me?"

"How?"

"I want you to tie me down."

"Tie you down?"

"With a couple of ropes. Just loosely, so I can turn if I want to. Do you mind?"

Her bare feet were already seeking her mules on the floor at her side of the bed. "All right," she sighed.

Roger Toomey sat in the small cubbyhole that passed for his office and stared at the pile of examination papers before him. At the moment, he didn't see how he was going to mark them.

He had given five lectures on electricity and magnetism since the first night he had floated. He had gotten through them somehow, though not swimmingly. The students asked ridiculous questions so probably he wasn't making himself as clear as he once did.

Today he had saved himself a lecture by giving a surprise

examination. He didn't bother making one up; just handed out copies of one given several years earlier.

Now he had the answer papers and would have to mark them. Why? Did it matter what they said? Or anyone? Was it so important to know the laws of physics? If it came to that, what were the laws? Were there any, really?

Or was it all just a mass of confusion out of which nothing orderly could ever be extracted? Was the universe, for all its appearance, merely the original chaos, still waiting for the Spriit to move upon the face of its deep?

Insomnia wasn't helping him, either. Even strapped in upon the couch, he slept only fitfully, and then always with dreams.

There was a knock at the door.

Roger cried angrily, "Who's there?"

A pause, and then the uncertain answer. "It's Miss Harroway, Dr. Toomey. I have the letters you dictated."

"Well, come in, come in. Don't just stand there."

The department secretary opened the door a minimum distance and squeezed her lean and unprepossessing body into his office. She had a sheaf of papers in her hand. To each was clipped a yellow carbon and a stamped, addressed envelope.

Roger was anxious to get rid of her. That was his mistake. He stretched forward to reach the letters as she approached and felt himself leave the chair.

He moved two feet forward, still in sitting position, before he could bring himself down hard, losing his balance and tumbling in the process. It was too late.

It was entirely too late. Miss Harroway dropped the letters in a fluttering handful. She screamed and turned, hitting the door with her shoulder, caroming out into the hall and dashing down the corridor in a clatter of high heels.

Roger rose, rubbing his aching hip. "Damn," he said forcefully.

But he couldn't help seeing her point. He pictured the sight as she must have seen it; a full-grown man, lifting smoothly out of his chair and gliding toward her in a maintained squat.

He picked up the letters and closed his office door. It was quite late in the day; the corridors would be empty; she would probably be quite incoherent. Still—he waited anxiously for the crowd to gather.

Nothing happened. Perhaps she was lying somewhere in a dead faint. Roger felt it a point of honor to seek her out and do what he could for her, but he told his conscience to go to the devil. Until he found out exactly what was wrong with him, exactly what this

34

wild nightmare of his was all about, he must do nothing to reveal it.

Nothing, that is, more than he had done already.

He leafed through the letters; one to every major theoretical physicist in the country. Home talent was insufficient for this sort of thing.

He wondered if Miss Harroway grasped the contents of the letters. He hoped not. He had couched them deliberately in technical language; more so, perhaps, than was quite necessary. Partly, that was to be discreet; partly, to impress the addressees with the fact that he, Toomey, was a legitimate and capable scientist.

One by one, he put the letters in the appropriate envelopes. The best brains in the country, he thought. Could they help?

He didn't know.

The library was quiet. Roger Toomey closed the *Journal of Theoretical Physics*, placed it on end and stared at its backstrap somberly. The *Journal of Theoretical Physics!* What did any of the contributors to that learned bit of balderdash understand anyway? The thought tore at him. Until so recently they had been the greatest men in the world to him.

And still he was doing his best to live up to their code and philosophy. With Jane's increasingly reluctant help, he had made measurements. He had tried to weigh the phenomenon in the balance, extract its relationships, evaluate its quantities. He had tried, in short, to defeat it in the only way he knew how—by making of it just another expression of the eternal modes of behavior that all the Universe must follow.

(*Must* follow. The best minds said so.)

Only there was nothing to measure. There was absolutely no sensation of effort to his levitation. Indoors—he dare not test himself outdoors, of course—he could reach the ceiling as easily as he could rise an inch, except that it took more time. Given enough time he felt, he could continue rising indefinitely; go to the Moon, if necessary.

He could carry weights while levitating. The process became slower, but there was no increase in effort.

The day before he had come on Jane without warning, a stopwatch in one hand.

"How much do you weigh?" he asked.

"One hundred ten," she replied. She gazed at him uncertainly. He seized her wrist with one arm. She tried to push him away but he paid no attention. Together, they moved upward at a creeping pace. She clung to him, white and rigid with terror.

"Twenty-two minutes thirteen seconds," he said, when his head nudged the ceiling.

When they came down again, Jane tore away and hurried out of the room.

Some days before he had passed a drugstore scale, standing shabbily on a street corner. The street was empty, so he stepped on and put in his penny. Even though he suspected something of the sort, it was a shock to find himself weighing thirty pounds.

He began carrying handfuls of pennies and weighing himself under all conditions. He was heavier on days on which there was a brisk wind, as though he required weight to keep from blowing away.

Adjustment was automatic. Whatever it was that levitated him maintained a balance between comfort and safety. But he could enforce conscious control upon his levitation just as he could upon his respiration. He could stand on a scale and force the pointer up to almost his full weight and down, of course, to nothing.

He bought a scale two days before and tried to measure the rate at which he could change weight. That didn't help. The rate whatever it was, was faster than the pointer could swing. All he did was collect data on moduli of compressibility and moments of inertia.

Well—What did it all amount to anyway?

He stood up and trudged out of the library, shoulders drooping. He touched tables and chairs as he walked to the side of the room and then kept his hand unobtrusively on the wall. He had to do that, he felt. Contact with matter kept him continually informed as to his status with respect to the ground. If his hand lost touch with a table or slid upward against the wall—That was it.

The corridor had the usual sprinkling of students. He ignored them. In these last days, they had gradually learned to stop greeting him. Roger imagined that some had come to think of him as queer and most were probably growing to dislike him.

He passed by the elevator. He never took it any more; going down, particularly. When the elevator made its initial drop, he found it impossible not to lift into the air for just a moment. No matter how he lay in wait for the moment, he hopped and people would turn and look at him.

He reached for the railing at the head of the stairs and just before his hand touched it, one of his feet kicked the other. It was

36

the most ungainly stumble that could be imagined. Three weeks earlier, Roger would have sprawled down the stairs.

This time his automatic system took over and, leaning forward, spread-eagled, fingers wide, legs half-buckled, he sailed down the flight gliderlike. He might have been on wires.

He was too dazed to right himself, too paralyzed with horror to do anything. Within two feet of the window at the bottom of the flight, he came to an automatic halt and hovered.

There were two students on the flight he had come down, both now pressed against the wall, three more at the head of the stairs, two on the flight below, and one on the landing with him, so close they could almost touch one another.

It was very silent. They all looked at him.

Roger straightened himself, dropped to the ground and ran down the stairs, pushing one student roughly out of his way.

Conversation swirled up into exclamation behind him.

"Dr. Morton wants to see me?" Roger turned in his chair, holding one of its arms firmly.

The new department secretary nodded. "Yes, Dr. Toomey."

She left quickly. In the short time since Miss Harroway had resigned, she had learned that Dr. Toomey had something "wrong" with him. The students avoided him. In his lecture room today, the back seats had been full of whispering students. The front seats had been empty.

Roger looked into the small wall mirror near the door. He adjusted his jacket and brushed some lint off but that operation did little to improve his appearance. His complexion had grown sallow. He had lost at least ten pounds since all this had started, though, of course, he had no way of really knowing his exact weight-loss. He was generally unhealthy-looking, as though his digestion perpetually disagreed with him and won every argument.

He had no apprehensions about this interview with the chairman of the department. He had reached a pronounced cynicism concerning the levitation incidents. Apparently, witnesses didn't talk. Miss Harroway hadn't. There was no sign that the students on the staircase had.

With a last touch at his tie, he left his office.

Dr. Philip Morton's office was not too far down the hall which was a gratifying fact to Roger. More and more, he was cultivating the habit of walking with systematic slowness. He picked up one foot and put it before him, watching. Then he picked up the other

37

and put it before him, still watching. He moved along in a confirmed stoop, gazing at his feet.

Dr. Morton frowned as Roger walked in. He had little eyes, wore a poorly-trimmed grizzled mustache and an untidy suit. He had a moderate reputation in the scientific world and a decided penchant for leaving teaching duties ot the members of his staff.

He said, "Say, Toomey, I got the strangest letter from Linus Deering. Did you write to him on"—he consulted a paper on his desk—"the twenty-second of last month. Is this your signature?"

Roger looked and nodded. Anxiously, he tried to read Deering's letter upside down. This was unexpected. Of the letters he had sent out the day of the Miss Harroway incident, only four had so far been answered.

Three of them had consisted of cold one-paragraph replies that read, more or less: "This is to acknowledge receipt of your letter of the 22nd. I do not believe I can help you in the matter you discuss." A fourth, from Ballantine of Northwestern Tech, had bumblingly suggested an institute for psychic research. Roger couldn't tell whether he was trying to be helpful or insulting.

Deering of Princeton made five. He had had hopes of Deering.

Dr. Morton cleared his throat loudly and adjusted a pair of glasses. "I want to read you what he says. Sit down, Toomey, sit down. He says: 'Dear Phil—'"

Dr. Morton looked up briefly with a slight, fatuous smile. "Linus and I met at Federation meetings last year. We had a few drinks together. Very nice fellow."

He adjusted his glasses again and returned to the letter: " 'Dear Phil: Is there a Dr. Roger Toomey in your department? I received a very queer letter from him the other day. I didn't quite know what to make of it. At first, I thought I'd let it go as another crank letter. Then I thought that since the letter carried your department heading, you ought to know of it. It's just possible someone may be using your staff as part of a confidence game. I'm enclosing Dr. Toomey's letter for your inspection. I hope to be visiting your part of the country—'

"Well the rest is personal." Dr. Morton folded the letter, took off his glasses, put them in a leather container and put that in his breast pocket. He twined his fingers together and leaned forward.

"Now," he said, "I don't have to read you your own letter. Was it a joke? A hoax?"

"Dr. Morton," said Roger, heavily, "I was serious. I don't see anything wrong with my letter. I sent it to quite a few physicists.

38

It speaks for itself. I've made observations on a case of . . . of levitation and I wanted information about possible theoretical explanations for such a phenomenon."

"Levitation! Really!"

"It's a legitimate case, Dr. Morton."

"You've observed it yourself?"

"Of course."

"No hidden wires? No mirrors? Look here, Toomey, you're no expert on these frauds."

"This was a thoroughly scientific series of observations. There is no possibility of fraud."

"You might have consulted me, Toomey, before sending out these letters."

"Perhaps I should have, Dr. Morton, but, frankly, I thought you might be—unsympathetic."

"Well, thank you. I should hope so. And on department stationery. I'm really surprised, Toomey. Look here, Toomey, your life is your own. If you wish to believe in levitation, go ahead, but strictly on your own time. For the sake of the department and the College, it should be obvious that this sort of thing should not be injected into your scholastic affairs.

"In point of fact, you've lost some weight recently, haven't you, Toomey? Yes, you don't look well at all. I'd see a doctor, it I were you. A nerve specialist, perhaps."

Roger said, bitterly, "A psychiatrist might be better, you think?"

"Well, that's entirely your business. In any case, a little rest—"

The telephone had rung and the secretary had taken the call. She caught Dr. Morton's eye and he picked up his extension.

He said, "Hello . . . Oh, Dr. Smithers, yes . . . Um-m-m . . . Yes. . . . Concerning whom? . . . Well, in point of fact, he's with me right now. . . . Yes. . . . Yes, immediately."

He cradled the phone and looked at Roger thoughtfully. "The dean wants to see both of us."

"What about, sir?"

"He didn't say." He got up and stepped to the door. "Are you coming, Toomey?"

"Yes, sir." Roger rose slowly to his feet, cramming the toe of one foot carefully under Dr. Morton's desk as he did so.

Dean Smithers was a lean man with a long, ascetic face. He had a mouthful of false teeth that fitted just badly enough to give his sibilants a peculiar half-whistle.

"Close the door, Miss Bryce," he said, "and I'll take no phone calls for a while. Sit down, gentlemen."

He stared at them portentously and added, "I think I had better get right to the point. I don't know exactly what Dr. Toomey is doing, but he must stop."

Dr. Morton turned upon Roger in amazement. "What have you been doing?"

Roger shrugged dispiritedly. "Nothing that I can help." He had underestimated student tongue-wagging after all.

"Oh, come, come." The dean registered impatience. "I'm sure I don't know how much of the story to discount, but it seems you must have been engaging in parlor tricks; silly parlor tricks quite unsuited to the spirit and dignity of this institution."

Dr. Morton said, "This is all beyond me."

The dean frowned. "It seems you haven't heard, then. It is amazing to me how the faculty can remain in complete ignorance of matters that fairly saturate the student body. I had never realized it before. I myself heard of it by accident; by a very fortunate accident, in fact, since I was able to intercept a newspaper reporter who arrived this morning looking for someone he called 'Dr. Toomey, the flying professor.' "

"What?" cried Dr. Morton.

Roger listened haggardly.

"That's what the reporter said. I quote him. It seems one of our students had called the paper. I ordered the newspaperman out and had the student sent to my office. According to him, Dr. Toomey flew—I use the word, 'flew,' because that's what the student insisted on calling it—down a flight of stairs and then back up again. He claimed there were a dozen witnesses."

"I went down the stairs only," muttered Roger.

Dean Smithers was tramping up and down along his carpet now. He had worked himself up into a feverish eloquence. "Now mind you, Toomey, I have nothing against amateur theatricals. In my stay in office I have constantly fought against stuffiness and false dignity. I have encouraged friendliness between ranks in the faculty and have not even objected to reasonable fraternization with students. So I have no objection to your putting on a show for the students *in your own home.*

"Surely you see what could happen to the College once an irresponsible press is done with us. Shall we have a flying professor craze succeed the flying saucer craze? If the reporters get in touch with you, Dr. Toomey, I will expect you to deny all such reports categorically."

40

"I understand, Dean Smithers."

"I trust we shall escape this incident without lasting damage. I must ask you, with all the firmness at my command, never to repeat your . . . uh . . . performance. If you ever do, your resignation will be requested. Do you understand, Dr. Toomey?"

"Yes," said Roger.

"In that case, good day, gentlemen."

Dr. Morton steered Roger back into his office. This time, he shooed his secretary and closed the door behind her carefully.

"Good heavens, Toomey," he whispered, "has this madness any connection with your letter on levitation?"

Roger's nerves were beginning to twang. "Isn't it obvious? I was referring to myself in those letters."

"You can fly? I mean, levitate?"

"Either word you choose."

"I never heard of such—Damn it, Toomey, did Miss Harroway ever see you levitate?"

"Once. It was an accid—"

"Of course. It's obvious now. She was so hysterical it was hard to make out. She said you had jumped at her. It sounded as though she were accusing you of . . . of—" Dr. Morton looked embarrassed. "Well, I didn't believe that. She was a good secretary, you understand, but obviously not one designed to attract the attention of a young man. I was actually relieved when she left. I thought she would be carrying a small revolver next, or accusing me—You . . . you levitated, eh?"

"Yes."

"How do you do it?"

Roger shook his head. "That's my problem. I don't know."

Dr. Morton allowed himself a smile. "Surely you don't repeal the law of gravity?"

"You know, I think I do. There must be antigravity involved somehow."

Dr. Morton's indignation at having a joke taken seriously was marked. He said, "Look here, Toomey, this is nothing to laugh at."

"*Laugh* at. Great Scott, Dr. Morton, do I look as though I were laughing?"

"Well—You need a rest. No question about it. A little rest and this nonsense of yours will pass. I'm sure of it."

"It's not nonsense." Roger bowed his head a moment, then said, in a quieter tone. "I tell you what, Dr. Morton, would you like to

41

go in to this with me? In some way this will open new horizons in physical science. I don't know how it works; I just can't conceive of any solution. The two of us together—"

Dr. Morton's look of horror penetrated by that time.

Roger said, "I know it all sounds queer. But I'll demonstrate for you. It's perfectly legitimate. I wish it weren't."

"Now, now," Dr. Morton sprang from his seat. "Don't exert yourself. You need a rest badly. I don't think you should wait till June. You go home right now. I'll see that your salary comes through and I'll look after your course. I used to give it myself once, you know."

"Dr. Morton. This is important."

"I know. I know." Dr. Morton clapped Roger on the shoulder. "Still, my boy, you look under the weather. Speaking frankly, you look like hell. You need a long rest."

"I *can* levitate." Roger's voice was climbing again. "You're just trying to get rid of me because you don't believe me. Do you think I'm lying? What would be my motive?"

"You're exciting yourself needlessly, my boy. You let me make a phone call. I'll have someone take you home."

"I tell you I *can* levitate," shouted Roger.

Dr. Morton turned red. "Look, Toomey, let's not discuss it. I don't care if you fly up in the air right this minute."

"You mean seeing isn't believing as far as you're concerned?"

"Levitation? Of course not." The department chairman was bellowing. "If I saw you fly, I'd see an optometrist or a psychiatrist. I'd sooner believe myself insane than that the laws of physics—"

He caught himself, harumphed loudly. "Well, as I said, let's not discuss it. I'll just make this phone call."

"No need, sir. No need," said Roger. "I'll go. I'll take my rest. Good-by."

He walked out rapidly, moving more quickly than at any time in days. Dr. Morton, on his feet, hands flat on his desk, looked at his departing back with relief.

James Sarle, M.D. was in the living room when Roger arrived home. He was lighting his pipe as Roger stepped through the door, one large-knuckled hand enclosing the bowl. He shook out the match and his ruddy face crinkled into a smile.

"Hello, Roger. Resigning from the human race? Haven't heard from you in over a month."

His black eyebrows met above the bridge of his nose, giving

him a rather forbidding appearance that somehow helped him establish the proper atmosphere with his patients.

Roger turned to Jane, who sat buried in an armchair. As usual lately, she had a look of wan exhaustion on her face.

Roger said to her, "Why did you bring him here?"

"Hold it! Hold it, man," said Sarle. "Nobody brought me. I met Jane downtown this morning and invited myself here. I'm bigger than she is. She couldn't keep me out."

"Met her by coincidence, I suppose? Do you make appointments for all your coincidences?"

Sarle laughed, "Let's put it this way. She told me a little about what's been going on."

Jane said, wearily, "I'm sorry if you disapprove, Roger, but it was the first chance I had to talk to someone who would understand."

"What make you think he understands? Tell me Jim, do you believe her story?"

Sarle said, "It's not an easy thing to believe. You'll admit that. But I'm trying."

"All right, suppose I flew. Suppose I levitated right now. What would you do?"

"Faint, maybe. Maybe I'd say, 'Holy Pete.' Maybe I'd burst out laughing. Why don't you try, and then we'll see?"

Roger stared at him. "You really want to see it?"

"Why shouldn't I?"

"The ones that have seen it screamed or ran or froze with horror. Can you take it, Jim?"

"I think so."

"O.K." Roger slipped two feet upward and executed a slow tenfold *entrechat*. He remained in the air, toes pointed downwards, legs together, arms gracefully outstretched in bitter parody.

"Better than Nijinski, eh, Jim?"

Sarle did none of the things he suggested he might do. Except for catching his pipe as it dropped, he did nothing at all.

Jane had closed her eyes. Tears squeezed quietly through the lids.

Sarle said, "Come down, Roger."

Roger did so. He took a seat and said, "I wrote to physicists, men of reputation. I explained the situation in an impersonal way. I said I thought it ought to be investigated. Most of them ignored me. One of them wrote to old man Morton to ask if I were crooked or crazy."

"Oh, Roger," whispered Jane.

"You think that's bad? The dean called me into his office today. I'm to stop my parlor tricks, he says. It seems I had stumbled down the stairs and automatically levitated myself to safety. Morton says he wouldn't believe I could fly if he saw me in action. Seeing isn't believing in his case, he says, and orders me to take a rest. I'm not going back."

"Roger," said Jane, her eyes opening wide. "Are you serious?"

"I can't go back. I'm sick of them. Scientists!"

"But what will you do?"

"I don't know." Roger buried his head in his hands. He said in a muffled voice, "You tell me, Jim. You're the psychiatrist. Why won't they believe me?"

"Perhaps it's a matter of self protection, Roger," said Sarle, slowly. "People aren't happy with anything they can't understand. Even some centuries ago when many people *did* believe in the existence of extranatural abilities, like flying on broomsticks, for instance, it was almost always assumed that these powers originated with the forces of evil.

"People still think so. They may not believe literally in the devil, but they do think that what is strange is evil. They'll fight against believing in levitation—or be scared to death if the fact is forced down their throats. That's true, so let's face it."

Roger shook his head. "You're talking about people, and I'm talking about scientists."

"Scientists are people."

"You know what I mean. I have here a phenomenon. It isn't witchcraft. I haven't dealt with the devil. Jim, there must be a natural explanation. We don't know all there is to know about gravitation. We know hardly anything, really. Don't you suppose it's just barely conceivable that there is some biological method of nullifying gravity. Perhaps I am a mutation of some sort. I have a . . . well, call it a muscle . . . which can abolish gravity. At least it can abolish the effect of gravity on myself. Well, let's investigate it. Why sit on your hands? If we have anti-gravity, imagine what it will mean to the human race."

"Hold it, Rog," said Sarle. "Think about the matter a while. Why are *you* so unhappy about it? According to Jane, you were almost mad with fear the first day it happened, *before* you had any way of knowing that science was going to ignore you and that your superiors would be unsympathetic."

"That's right," murmured Jane.

Sarle said, "Now why should that be? Here you had a great,

new, wonderful power; a sudden freedom from the deadly pull of gravity."

Roger said, "Oh, don't be a fool. It was—horrible. I couldn't understand it. I still can't."

"Exactly, my boy. It was something you couldn't understand and *therefore* something horrible. You're a physical scientist. You *know* what makes the universe run. Or if you don't know, you know someone else knows. Even if no one understands a certain point, you know that some day someone will know. The key word is *know*. It's part of your life. Now you come face to face with a phenomenon which you consider to violate one of the basic laws of the universe. Scientists say: Two masses will attract one another according to a fixed mathematical rule. It is an inalienable property of matter and space. There are no exceptions. And now you're an exception."

Roger said, glumly, "And how."

"You see, Roger," Sarle went on, "for the first time in history, mankind really has what he considers unbreakable rules. I mean, unbreakable. In primitive cultures, a medicine man might use a spell to produce rain. If it didn't work, it didn't upset the validity of magic. It just meant that the shaman had neglected some part of his spell, or had broken a taboo, or offended a god. In modern theocratic cultures, the commandments of the Deity are unbreakable. Still if a man were to break the commandments and yet prosper, it would be no sign that that particular religion was invalid. The ways of Providence are admittedly mysterious and some invisible punishment awaits.

"Today, however, we have rules that *really* can't be broken, and one of them is the existence of gravity. It works even though the man who invokes it has forgotten to mutter em-em-over-ahr-square."

Roger managed a twisted smile. "You're all wrong, Jim. The unbreakable rules have been broken over and over again. Radioactivity was impossible when it was discovered. Energy came out of nowhere; incredible quantities of it. It was as ridiculous as levitation."

"Radioactivity was an objective phenomenon that could be communicated and duplicated. Uranium would fog photographic film for anyone. A Crookes tube could be built by anyone and would deliver an electron stream in identical fashion for all. You—"

"I've tried communicating—"

"I know. But can you tell me, for instance, how *I* might levitate."

45

"Of course not."

"That limits others to observation only without experimental duplication. It puts your levitation on the same plane with stellar evolution, something to theorize about but never experiment with."

"Yet scientists are willing to devote their lives to astrophysics."

"Scientists are people. They can't reach the stars, so they make the best of it. But they can reach you and to be unable to touch your levitation would be infuriating."

"Jim, they haven't even tried. You talk as though I've been studied. Jim, they won't even consider the problem."

"They don't have to. Your levitation is part of a whole class of phenomena that won't be considered. Telepathy, clairvoyance, prescience and a thousand other extra-natural powers are practically never seriously investigated, even though reported with every appearance of reliability. Rhine's experiments on E.S.P. have annoyed far more scientists than they have intrigued. So you see, they don't have to study you to know they don't want to study you. They know that in advance."

"Is this funny to you, Jim? Scientists refuse to investigate facts; they turn their back on the truth. And you just sit there and grin and make droll statements."

"No, Roger, I know it's serious. And I have no glib explanations for mankind, really. I'm giving you my thoughts. It's what I think. But don't you see? What I'm doing, really, is to try to look at things as they are. It's what you must do. Forget your ideals, your theories, your notions as to what people *ought* to do. Consider what they *are* doing. Once a person is orientated to face facts rather than delusions, problems tend to disappear. At the very least, they fall into their true perspective and become soluble."

Roger stirred restlessly. "Psychiatric gobbledygook! It's like putting your fingers on a man's temple and saying, 'Have faith and you will be cured!' If the poor chap isn't cured, it's because he didn't drum up enough faith. The witch doctor can't lose."

"Maybe you're right, but let's see. What *is* your problem?"

"No catechism, please. You know my problem so let's not horse around."

"You levitate. Is that it?"

"Let's say it is. It'll do as a first approximation."

"You're not being serious, Roger, but actually you're probably right. It's only a first approximation. After all you're tackling that problem. Jane tells me you've been experimenting."

"Experimenting! Ye Gods, Jim, I'm not experimenting. I'm

drifting. I need high-powered brains and equipment. I need a research team and I don't have it."

"Then what's your problem? Second approximation."

Roger said, "I see what you mean. My problem is to get a research team. But I've tried! Man, I've tried till I'm tired of trying."

"How have you tried?"

"I've sent out letters. I've asked—Oh, stop it, Jim. I haven't the heart to go through the patient-on-the-couch routine. You know what I've been doing."

"I know that you've said to people, 'I have a problem. Help me.' Have you tried anything else?"

"Look, Jim. I'm dealing with mature scientists."

"I know. So you reason that the straightforward request is sufficient. Again it's theory against fact. I've told you the difficulties involved in your request. When you thumb a ride on a highway you're making a straightforward request, but most cars pass you by just the same. The point is that the straightforward request has failed. Now what's your problem? Third approximation!"

"To find another approach which won't fail? Is that what you want me to say?"

"It's what you have said, isn't it?"

"So I know it without your telling me."

"Do you? You're ready to quit school, quit your job, quit science. Where's your consistency, Rog? Do you abandon a problem when your first experiment fails? Do you give up when one theory is shown to be inadequate? The same philosophy of experimental science that holds for inanimate objects should hold for people as well."

"All right. What do you suggest I try? Bribery? Threats? Tears?"

James Sarle stood up. "Do you really want a suggestion?"

"Go ahead."

"Do as Dr. Morton said. Take a vacation and to hell with levitation. It's a problem for the future. Sleep in bed and float or don't float; what's the difference. Ignore levitation. laugh at it or even enjoy it. Do anything but worry about it, because it isn't your problem. That's the whole point. It's not your immediate problem. Spend your time considering how to make scientists study something they don't want to study. That is the immediate problem and that is exactly what you've spent no thinking time on as yet."

Sarle walked to the hall closet and got his coat. Roger went with him. Minutes passed in silence.

Then Roger said without looking up, "Maybe you're right, Jim."

"Maybe I am. Try it and then tell me. Good-by, Roger."

Roger Toomey opened his eyes and blinked at the morning brightness of the bedroom. He called out, "Hey, Jane, where are you?"

Jane's voice answered, "In the kitchen. Where do you think?"

"Come in here, will you?"

She came in. "The bacon won't fry itself, you know."

"Listen, did I float last night?"

"I don't know. I slept."

"You're a help." He got out of bed and slipped his feet into his mules. "Still I don't think I did."

"Do you think you've forgotten how?" There was sudden hope in her voice.

"I haven't forgotten. See!" He slid into the dining room on a cushion of air. "I just have a feeling I haven't floated. I think it's three nights now."

"Well, that's good," said Jane. She was back at the stove. "It's just that a month's rest has done you good. If I had called Jim in the beginning—"

"Oh, please, don't go through that. A month's rest, my eye. It's just that last Sunday I made up my mind what to do. Since then I've relaxed. That's all there is to it."

"What are you going to do?"

"Every spring Northwestern Tech gives a series of seminars on physical topics. I'll attend."

"You mean, go way out to Seattle."

"Of course."

"What will they be discussing?"

"What's the difference? I just want to see Linus Deering."

"But he's the one who called you crazy, isn't he?"

"He did." Roger scooped up a forkful of scrambled eggs. "But he's also the best man of the lot."

He reached for the salt and lifted a few inches out of his chair as he did so. He paid no attention.

He said, "I think maybe I can handle him."

The spring seminars at Northwestern Tech had become a nationally known institution since Linus Deering had joined the

48

faculty. He was the perennial chairman and lent the proceedings their distinctive tone. He introduced the speakers, led the questioning periods, summed up at the close of each morning and afternoon session and was the soul of conviviality at the concluding dinner at the end of the week's work.

All this Roger Toomey knew by report. He could now observe the actual workings of the man. Professor Deering was rather under the middle height, was dark of complexion and had a luxuriant and quite distinctive mop of wavy brown hair. His wide thin-lipped mouth when not engaged in active conversation looked perpetually on the point of a sly smile. He spoke quickly and fluently, without notes, and seemed always to deliver his comments from a level of superiority that his listeners automatically accepted.

At least, so he had been on the first morning of the seminar. It was only during the afternoon session that the listeners began to notice a certain hesitation in his remarks. Even more, there was an uneasiness about him as he sat on the stage during the delivery of the scheduled papers. Occasionally, he glanced furtively toward the rear of the auditorium.

Roger Toomey, seated in the very last row, observed all this tensely. His temporary glide toward normality that had begun when he first thought there might be a way out was beginning to recede.

On the Pullman to Seattle, he had not slept. He had had visions of himself lifting upward in time to the wheel-clacking, of moving out quietly past the curtains and into the corridor, of being awakened into endless embarrassment by the hoarse shouting of a porter. So he had fastened the curtains with safety pins and had achieved nothing by that; no feeling of security; no sleep outside a few exhausting snatches.

He had napped in his seat during the day, while the mountains slipped past outside, and arrived in Seattle in the evening with a stiff neck, aching bones, and a general sensation of despair.

He had made his decision to attend the seminar far too late to have been able to obtain a room to himself at the Institute's dormitories. Sharing a room was, of course, quite out of the question. He registered at a downtown hotel, locked the door, closed and locked all the windows, shoved his bed hard against the wall and the bureau against the open side of the bed; then slept.

He remembered no dreams, and when he awoke in the morning he was still lying within the manufactured enclosure. He felt relieved.

When he arrived, in good time, at Physics Hall on the Institute's campus, he found, as he expected, a large room and a small gathering. The seminar sessions were held, traditionally, over the Easter vacation and students were not in attendance. Some fifty physicists sat in the auditorium designed to hold four hundred, clustering on either side of the central aisle up near the podium.

Roger took his seat in the last row, where he would not be seen by casual passers-by looking through the high, small windows of the auditorium door, and where the others in the audience would have had to twist through nearly a hundred and eighty degrees to see him.

Except, of course, for the speaker on the platform—and for Professor Deering.

Roger did not hear much of the actual proceedings. He concentrated entirely on waiting for those moments when Deering was alone on the platform; when only Deering could see him.

As Deering grew obviously more disturbed, Roger grew bolder. During the final summing up of the afternoon, he did his best.

Professor Deering stopped altogether in the middle of a poorly-constructed and entirely meaningless sentence. His audience, which had been shifting in their seats for some time stopped also and looked wonderingly at him.

Deering raised his hand and said, gaspingly, "You! You there!"

Roger Toomey had been sitting with an air of complete relaxation—in the very center of the aisle. The only chair beneath him was composed of two and a half feet of empty air. His legs were stretched out before him on the armrest of an equally airy chair.

When Deering pointed, Roger slid rapidly sidewise. By the time fifty heads turned, he was sitting quietly in a very prosaic wooden seat.

Roger looked this way and that, then stared at Deering's pointing finger and rose.

"Are you speaking to me, Professor Deering?" he asked, with only the slightest tremble in his voice to indicate the savage battle he was fighting within himself to keep that voice cool and wondering.

"What are you doing?" demanded Deering, his morning's tension exploding.

Some of the audience were standing in order to see better. An unexpected commotion is as dearly loved by a gathering of research physicists as by a crowd at a baseball game.

"I'm not doing anything," said Roger. " I don't understand you."

"Get out! Leave this hall!"

Deering was beside himself with a mixture of emotions, or perhaps he would not have said that. At any rate, Roger sighed and took his opportunity prayerfully.

He said, loudly and distinctly, forcing himself to be heard over the gathering clamor, "I am Professor Roger Toomey of Carson College. I am a member of the American Physical Association. I have applied for permission to attend these sessions, have been accepted, and have paid my registration fee. I am sitting here as is my right and will continue to do so."

Deering could only say blindly, "Get out!"

"I will not," said Roger. He was actually trembling with a synthetic and self-imposed anger. "For what reason must I get out? What have I done?"

Deering put a shaking hand through his hair. He was quite unable to answer.

Roger followed up his advantage. "If you attempt to evict me from these sessions without just cause, I shall certainly sue the Institute."

Deering said, hurriedly, "I call the first day's session of the Spring Seminars of Recent Advances in the Physical Sciences to a close. Our next session will be in this hall tomorrow at nine in—"

Roger left as he was speaking and hurried away.

There was a knock at Roger's hotelroom door that night. It startled him, froze him in his chair.

"Who is it?" he cried.

The answering voice was soft and hurried. "May I see you?"

It was Deering's voice. Roger's hotel as well as his room number were, of course, recorded with the seminar secretary. Roger had hoped, but scarcely expected, that the day's events would have so speedy a consequence.

He opened the door, said stiffly, "Good evening, Professor Deering."

Deering stepped in and looked about. He wore a very light topcoat that he made no gesture to remove. He held his hat in his hand and did not offer to put it down.

He said, "Professor Roger Toomey of Carson College. Right?" He said it with a certain emphasis, as though the name had significance.

"Yes. Sit down, professor."

Deering remained standing. "Now what is it? What are you after?"

"I don't understand."

"I'm sure you do. You aren't arranging this ridiculous foolery for nothing. Are you trying to make me seem foolish or is it that you expect to hoodwink me into some crooked scheme. I want you to know it won't work. And don't try to use force now. I have friends who know exactly where I am at this moment. I'll advise you to tell the truth and then get out of town."

"Professor Deering! This is my room. If you are here to bully me, I'll ask you to leave. If you don't go, I'll have you put out."

"Do you intend to continue this ... this persecution?"

"I have not been persecuting you. I don't know you, sir."

"Aren't you the Roger Toomey who wrote me a letter concerning a case of levitation he wanted me to investigate?"

Roger stared at the man. "What letter is this?"

"Do you deny it?"

"Of course I do. What are you talking about? Have you got the letter?"

Professor Deering's lips compressed. "Never mind that. Do you deny you were suspending yourself on wires at this afternoon's sessions?"

"On wires? I don't follow you at all."

"You were levitating!"

"Would you please leave, Professor Deering? I don't think you're well."

The physicist raised his voice. "Do you deny you were levitating?"

"I think you're mad. Do you mean to say I made magician's arrangements in your auditorium. I was never in it before today and when I arrived you were already present. Did you find wires or anything of the sort after I left?"

"I don't know how you did it and I don't care. *Do* you deny you were levitating?"

"Why, of course I do."

"I saw you. Why are you lying?"

"You saw me levitate? Professor Deering, will you tell me how that's possible? I suppose your knowledge of gravitational forces is enough to tell you that true levitation is a meaningless concept except in outer space. Are you playing some sort of joke on me?"

"Good heavens," said Deering in a shrill voice, "why won't you tell me the truth?"

"I am. Do you suppose that by stretching out my hand and making a mystic pass ... so ... I can go sailing off into air." And Roger did so, his head brushing the ceiling.

Deering's head jerked upward, "Ah! There . . . there—"

Roger returned to earth, smiling. "You *can't* be serious."

"You did it again. You just did it."

"Did what, sir?"

"You levitated. You just levitated. You can't deny it."

Roger's eyes grew serious. "I think you're sick, sir."

"I know what I saw."

"Perhaps you need a rest. Overwork—"

"It was *not* a hallucination."

"Would you care for a drink?" Roger walked to his suitcase while Deering followed his footsteps with bulging eyes. The toes of his shoes touched air two inches from the ground and went no lower.

Deering sank into the chair Roger had vacated.

"Yes, please," he said, weakly.

Roger gave him the whiskey bottle, watched the other drink, then gag a bit. "How do you feel now?"

"Look here," said Deering, "have you discovered a way of neutralizing gravity?"

Roger stared. "Get hold of yourself, professor. If I had anti-gravity, I wouldn't use it to play games on you. I'd be in Washington. I'd be a military secret. I'd be— Well, I wouldn't be here! Surely all this is obvious to you?"

Deering jumped to his feet. "Do you intend sitting in on the remaining sessions?"

"Of course."

Deering nodded, jerked his hat down upon his head and hurried out.

For the next three days, Professor Deering did not preside over the seminar sessions. No reason for his absence was given. Roger Toomey, caught between hope and apprehension, sat in the body of the audience and tried to remain inconspicuous. In this, he was not entirely successful. Deering's public attack had made him notorious while his own strong defense had given him a kind of David versus Goliath popularity.

Roger returned to his hotel room Thursday night after an unsatisfactory dinner and remained standing in the doorway, one foot over the threshold. Professor Deering was gazing at him from within. And another man, a gray fedora shoved well back on his forehead, was seated on Roger's bed.

It was the stranger who spoke. "Come inside, Toomey."

Roger did so. "What's going on?"

The stranger opened his wallet and presented a cellophane window to Roger. He said, "I'm Cannon of the F.B.I."

Roger said, "You have influence with the government, I take it, Professor Deering."

"A little," said Deering.

Roger said, "Well, am I under arrest? What's my crime?"

"Take it easy," said Cannon. "We've been collecting some data on you, Toomey. Is this your signature?"

He held a letter out far enough for Roger to see, but not to snatch. It was the letter Roger had written to Deering which the latter had sent on to Morton.

"Yes," said Roger.

"How about this one?" The federal agent had a sheaf of letters.

Roger realized that he must have collected every one he had sent out, minus those that had been torn up. "They're all mine," he said, wearily.

Deering snorted.

Cannon said, "Professor Deering tells us that you can float."

"Float? What the devil do you mean, float?"

"Float in the air," said Cannon, stolidly.

"Do you believe anything as crazy as that?"

"I'm not here to believe or not to believe, Dr. Toomey," said Cannon. "I'm an agent of the Government of the United States and I've got an assignment to carry out. I'd co-operate if I were you."

"How can I co-operate in something like this? If I came to you and told you that Professor Deering could float in air, you'd have me flat on a psychiatrist's couch in no time."

Cannon said, "Professor Deering has been examined by a psychiatrist at his own request. However, the government has been in the habit of listening very seriously to Professor Deering for a number of years now. Besides, I might as well tell you that we have independent evidence."

"Such as?"

"A group of students at your college have seen you float. Also, a woman who was once secretary to the head of your department. We have statements from all of them."

Roger said, "What kind of statements? Sensible ones that you would be willing to put into the record and show to my congressman?"

Professor Deering interrupted anxiously, "Dr. Toomey, what do you gain by denying the fact that you can levitate? Your own dean admits that you've done something of the sort. He has told

54

me that he will inform you officially that your appointment will be terminated at the end of the academic year. He wouldn't do that for nothing."

"That doesn't matter," said Roger.

"But why won't you admit I saw you levitate?"

"Why should I?"

Cannon said, "I'd like to point out, Dr. Toomey, that if you have any device for counteracting gravity, it would be of great importance to your government."

"Really? I suppose you have investigated my background for possible disloyalty."

"The investigation," said the agent, "is proceeding."

"All right," said Roger, "let's take a hypothetical case. Suppose I admitted I could levitate. Suppose I didn't know how I did it. Suppose I had nothing to give the government but my body and an insoluble problem."

"How can you know it's insoluble?" asked Deering, eagerly.

"I once asked you to study such a phenomenon," pointed out Roger, mildly. "You refused."

"Forget that. Look," Deering spoke rapidly, urgently. "You don't have a position at the moment. I can offer you one in my department as Associate Professor of Physics. Your teaching duties will be nominal. Full time research on levitation. What about it?"

"It sounds attractive," said Roger.

"I think it's safe to say that unlimited government funds will be available."

"What do I have to do? Just admit I can levitate?"

"I know you can. I saw you. I want you to do it now for Mr. Cannon."

Roger's legs moved upward and his body stretched out horizontally at the level of Cannon's head. He turned to one side and seemed to rest on his right elbow.

Cannon's hat fell backward onto the bed.

He yelled: "He floats."

Deering was almost incoherent with excitement. "Do you see it, man?"

"I sure see something."

"Then report it. Put it right down in your report, do you hear me? Make a complete record of it. They won't say there's anything wrong with me. I didn't doubt for a minute that I had seen it."

But he couldn't have been so happy if that were entirely true.

"I don't even know what the climate is like in Seattle," wailed Jane, "and there are a million things I have to do."

"Need any help?" asked Jim Sarle from his comfortable position in the depths of the armchair.

"There's nothing you can do. Oh, dear." And she flew from the room, but unlike her husband, she did so figuratively only.

Roger Toomey came in. "Jane, do we have the crates for the books yet? Hello, Jim. When did you come in? And where's Jane?"

"I came in a minute ago and Jane's in the next room. I had to get past a policeman to get in. Man, they've got you surrounded."

"Um-m-m," said Roger, absently. "I told them about you."

"I know you did. I've been sworn to secrecy. I told them it was a matter of professional confidence in any case. Why don't you let the movers do the packing? The government is paying, isn't it?"

"Movers wouldn't do it right," said Jane, suddenly hurrying in again and flouncing down on the sofa. "I'm going to have a cigarette."

"Break down, Roger," said Sarle, "and tell me what happened."

Roger smiled sheepishly. "As you said, Jim, I took my mind off the wrong problem and applied it to the right one. It just seemed to me that I was forever being faced with two alternatives. I was either crooked or crazy. Deering said that flatly in his letter to Morton. The dean assumed I was crooked and Morton suspected that I was crazy.

"But supposing I could show them that I could really levitate. Well, Morton told me what would happen in that case. Either I would be crooked or the *witness* would be insane. Morton said that . . . he said that if he saw me fly, he'd prefer to believe himself insane than accept the evidence. Of course, he was only being rhetorical. No man would believe in his own insanity while even the faintest alternative existed. I counted on that.

"So I changed my tactics. I went to Deering's seminar. I didn't *tell* him I could float; I showed him, *and then denied I had done it.* The alternative was clear. I was either lying or he . . . not I, mind you, but *he* . . . was mad. It was obvious that he would sooner believe in levitation than doubt his own sanity, once he was really put to the test. All his actions thereafter; his bullying, his trip to Washington, his offer of a job, were all intended only to vindicate his own sanity, not to help me."

Sarle said, "In other words you had made your levitation his problem and not your own."

Roger said, "Did you have anything like this in mind when we had our talk, Jim?"

Sarle shook his head. "I had vague notions but a man must solve his own problems if they're to be solved effectively. Do you think they'll work out the principle of levitation now?"

"I don't know, Jim. I still can't communicate the subjective aspects of the phenomenon. But that doesn't matter. We'll be investigating them and that's what counts." He struck his balled right fist into the palm of his left hand. "As far as I'm concerned the important point is that I made them help me."

"Is it?" asked Sarle, softly. "I should say that the important point is that you let them make *you* help *them*, which is a different thing altogether."

Breeds There a Man . . . ?

Police Sergeant Mankiewicz was on the telephone and he wasn't enjoying it. His conversation was sounding like a one-sided view of a firecracker.

He was saying, "That's right! He came in here and said, 'Put me in jail, because I want to kill myself.'

". . . I can't help that. Those were his exact words. It sounds crazy to me, too.

". . . Look, mister, the guy answers the description. You asked me for information and I'm giving it to you.

". . . He has exactly that scar on his right cheek and he said his name was John Smith. He didn't say it was Doctor anything-at-all.

". . . Well, sure it's a phony. Nobody is named John Smith. Not in a police station, anyway.

". . . He's in jail now.

". . . Yes, I mean it.

". . . Resisting an officer; assault and battery; malicious mischief. That's three counts.

". . . I don't care who he is.

". . . All right. I'll hold on."

He looked up at Officer Brown and put his hand over the mouthpiece of the phone. It was a ham of a hand that nearly swallowed up the phone altogether. His blunt-featured face was ruddy and steaming under a thatch of pale-yellow hair.

He said, "Trouble! Nothing but trouble at a precinct station. I'd rather be pounding the beat any day."

"Who's on the phone?" asked Brown. He had just come in and didn't really care. He thought Mankiewicz would look better on a suburban beat, too.

"Oak Ridge. Long Distance. A guy called Grant. Head of the somethingological division, and now he's getting somebody else at seventy-five cents a min . . . Hello!"

Mankiewicz got a new grip on the phone and held himself down.

"Look," he said, "let me go through this from the beginning. I want you to get it straight and then if you don't like it, you can send someone down here. The guy doesn't want a lawyer. He claims he just wants to stay in jail and, brother, that's all right with me.

"Well, will you listen? He came in yesterday, walked right up to me, and said, 'Officer, I want you to put me in jail because I want to kill myself.' So I said, 'Mister, I'm sorry you want to kill yourself. Don't do it, because if you do, you'll regret it the rest of your life.'

". . . I *am* serious. I'm just telling you what I said. I'm not saying it was a funny joke, but I've got my own troubles here, if you know what I mean. Do you think all I've got to do here is to listen to cranks who walk in and—

". . . Give me a chance, will you? I said, 'I can't put you in jail for wanting to kill yourself. That's no crime.' And he said, 'But I don't want to die.' So I said, 'Look, bud, get out of here.' I mean if a guy wants to commit suicide, all right, and if he doesn't want to, all right, but I don't want him weeping on my shoulder.

". . . I'm *getting* on with it. So he said to me, 'If I commit a crime, will you put me in jail?' I said, 'If you're caught and if someone files a charge and you can't put up bail, we will. Now beat it.' So he picked up the inkwell on my desk and before I could stop him, he turned it upside down on the open police blotter.

". . . That's right! Why do you think we have 'malicious mischief' tabbed on him? The ink ran down all over my pants.

". . . Yes, assault and battery, too! I came hopping down to shake a little sense into him, and he kicked me in the shins and handed me one in the eye.

". . . I'm not making this up. You want to come down here and look at my face?

". . . He'll be up in court one of these days. About Thursday, maybe.

". . . Ninety days is the least he'll get, unless the psychoes say otherwise. I think he belongs in the loony-bin myself.

". . . Officially, he's John Smith. That's the only name he'll give.

". . . No, sir, he doesn't get released without the proper legal steps.

". . . O.K., you do that, if you want to, bud! I just do my job here."

He banged the phone into its cradle, glowered at it, then picked it up again and began dialing. He said, "Gianetti?", got the proper answer and began talking:

59

"What's the A.E.C.? I've been talking to some Joe on the phone and he says—

". . . No, I'm not kidding, lunk-head. If I were kidding, I'd put up a sign. What's the alphabet soup?"

He listened, said, "Thanks" in a small voice, and hung up again.

He had lost some of his color. "That second guy was the head of the Atomic Energy Commission," he said to Brown. "They must have switched me from Oak Ridge to Washington."

Brown lounged to his feet, "Maybe the F.B.I. is after this John Smith guy. Maybe he's one of these here scientists." He felt moved to philosophy. "They ought to keep atomic secrets away from those guys. Things were O.K. as long as General Groves was the only fella who knew about the atom bomb. Once they cut in these here scientists on it, though—"

"Ah, shut up," snarled Mankiewicz.

Dr. Oswald Grant kept his eyes fixed on the white line that marked the highway and handled the car as though it were an enemy of his. He always did. He was tall and knobby with a withdrawn expression stamped on his face. His knees crowded the wheel, and his knuckles whitened whenever he made a turn.

Inspector Darrity sat beside him with his legs crossed so that the sole of his left shoe came up hard against the door. It would leave a sandy mark when he took it away. He tossed a nut-brown penknife from hand to hand. Earlier, he had unsheathed its wicked, gleaming blade and scraped casually at his nails as they drove, but a sudden swerve had nearly cost him a finger and he desisted.

He said, "What do you know about this Ralson?"

Dr. Grant took his eyes from the road momentarily, then returned them. He said, uneasily, "I've known him since he took his doctorate at Princeton. He's a very brilliant man."

"Yes? Brilliant, huh? Why is it that all you scientific men describe one another as 'brilliant'? Aren't there any mediocre ones?"

"Many. I'm one of them. But Ralson isn't. You ask anyone. Ask Oppenheimer. Ask Bush. He was the youngest observer at Alamogordo."

"O.K. He was brilliant. What about his private life?"

Grant waited, "I wouldn't know."

"You know him since Princeton. How many years is that?"

They had been scouring north along the highway from Washington for two hours with scarcely a word between them. Now Grant

60

felt the atmosphere change and the grip of the law on his coat collar.

"He got it in '43."

"You've known him eight years then."

"That's right."

"And you don't know about his private life?"

"A man's life is his own, inspector. He wasn't very sociable. A great many of the men are like that. They work under pressure and when they're off the job, they're not interested in continuing the lab acquaintanceships."

"Did he belong to any organizations that you know of?"

"No."

The inspector said, "Did he ever say anything to you that might indicate he was disloyal?"

Grant shouted, "No!" and there was silence for a while.

Then Darrity said, "How important is Ralson in atomic research?"

Grant hunched over the wheel and said, "As important as any one man can be. I grant you that no one is indispensable, but Ralson has always seemed to be rather unique. He has the engineering mentality."

"What does that mean?"

"He isn't much of a mathematician himself, but he can work out the gadgets that put someone else's math into life. There's no one like him when it comes to that. Time and again, inspector, we've had a problem to lick and no time to lick it in. There were nothing but blank minds all around until he put some thought into it and said, 'Why don't you try so-and-so?' Then he'd go away. He wouldn't even be interested enough to see if it worked. But it always did. Always! Maybe we would have got it ourselves eventually, but it might have taken months of additional time. I don't know how he does it. It's no use asking him either. He just looks at you and says, 'It was obvious,' and walks away. Of course, once he's shown us how to do it, it *is* obvious."

The inspector let him have his say out. When no more came, said, "Would you say he was queer, mentally? Erratic, you know."

"When a person is a genius, you wouldn't expect him to be normal, would you?"

"Maybe not. But just how abnormal was this particular genius."

"He never talked, particularly. Sometimes, he wouldn't work."

"Stayed at home and went fishing instead?"

"No. He came to the labs all right; but he would just sit at his

61

desk. Sometimes that would go on for weeks. Wouldn't answer you, or even look at you, when you spoke to him."

"Did he ever actually leave work altogether?"

"Before now, you mean? Never!"

"Did he ever claim he wanted to commit suicide? Ever say he wouldn't feel safe except in jail?"

"No."

"You're sure this John Smith is Ralson."

"I'm almost positive. He has a chemical burn on his right cheek that can't be mistaken."

"O.K. That's that, then I'll speak to him and see what he sounds like."

The silence fell for good this time. Dr. Grant following the snaking line as Inspector Darrity tossed the penknife in low arcs from hand to hand.

The warden listened to the call-box and looked up at his visitors, "We can have him brought up here, inspector, regardless."

"No," Dr. Grant shook his head. "Let's go to him."

Darrity said, "Is that normal for Ralson, Dr. Grant? Would you expect him to attack a guard trying to take him out of a prison cell."

Grant said, "I can't say."

The warden spread a calloused palm. His thick nose twitched a little, "We haven't tried to do anything about him so far because of the telegram from Washington, but, frankly, he doesn't belong here. I'll be glad to have him taken off my hands."

"We'll see him in his cell," said Darrity.

They went down the hard, barlined corridor. Empty, incurious eyes watched their passing.

Dr. Grant felt his flesh crawl, "Has he been kept *here* all the time?"

Darrity did not answer.

The guard, pacing before them, stopped, "This is the cell."

Daritty said, "Is that Dr. Ralson?"

Dr. Grant looked silently at the figure upon the cot. The man had been lying down when they first reached the cell, but now he had risen to one elbow and seemed to be trying to shrink into the wall. His hair was sandy and thin, his figure slight, his eyes blank and china-blue. On his right cheek there was a raised pink patch that tailed off like a tadpole.

Dr. Grant said, "That's Ralson."

The guard opened the door and stepped inside, but Inspector

Darrity sent him out again with a gesture. Ralson watched them mutely. He had drawn both feet up to the cot and was pushing backwards. His Adam's apple bobbled as he swallowed.

Darrity said, quietly, "Dr. Elwood Ralson?"

"What do you want?" The voice was a surprising baritone.

"Would you come with us, please? We have some questions we would like to ask you."

"No! Leave me alone!"

"Dr. Ralson," said Grant. "I've been sent here to ask you to come back to work."

Ralson looked at the scientist and there was a momentary glint of something other than fear in his eyes. He said, "Hello, Grant." He got off his cot, "Listen, I've been trying to have them put me into a padded cell. Can't you make them do that for me? You know me, Grant. I wouldn't ask for something I didn't feel was necessary. Help me. I can't stand the hard walls. It makes me want to . . . bash—" He brought the flat of his palm thudding down against the hard dull-gray concrete behind his cot.

Darrity looked thoughtful. He brought out his penknife and unbent the gleaming blade. Carefully, he scraped at his thumbnail, and said, "Would you like to see a doctor?"

But Ralson didn't answer that. He followed the gleam of metal and his lips parted and grew wet. His breath became ragged and harsh.

He said, "Put that away!"

Darrity paused, "Put what away?"

"The knife. Don't hold it in front of me. I can't stand looking at it."

Darrity said, "Why not?" He held it out, "Anything wrong with it? It's a good knife."

Ralson lunged. Darrity stepped back and his left hand came down on the other's wrist. He lifted the knife high in the air, "What's the matter, Ralson? What are you after?"

Grant cried a protest but Darrity waved him away.

Darrity said, "What do you want, Ralson?"

Ralson tried to reach upward, and bent under the other's appalling grip. He gasped, "Give me the knife."

"Why, Ralson? What do you want to do with it?"

"Please. I've got to—" He was pleading, "I've got to stop living."

"You want to die?"

"No. But I must."

Darrity shoved. Ralson flailed backward and tumbled into his cot, so that it squeaked noisily. Slowly, Darrity bent the blade of his penknife into its sheath and put it away. Ralson covered his face. His shoulders were shaking but otherwise he did not move.

There was the sound of shouting from the corridor, as the other prisoners reacted to the noise issuing from Ralson's cell. The guard came hurrying down, yelling "Quiet!" as he went.

Darrity looked up, "It's all right, guard."

He was wiping his hands upon a large white handkerchief, "I think we'll get a doctor for him."

Dr. Gottfried Blaustein was small and dark and spoke with a trace of an Austrian accent. He needed only a small goatee to be the layman's caricature of a psychiatrist. But he was clean-shaven, and very carefully dressed. He watched Grant carefully, assessing him, blocking in certain observations and deductions. He did this automatically, now, with everyone he met.

He said, "You give me a sort of picture. You describe a man of great talent, perhaps even genius. You tell me he has always been uncomfortable with people; that he has never fitted in with his laboratory environment, even though it was there that he met the greatest of success. Is there another environment to which he has fitted himself?"

"I don't understand."

"It is not given to all of us to be so fortunate as to find a congenial type of company at the place or in the field where we find it necessary to make a living. Often, one compensates by playing an instrument, or going hiking, or joining some club. In other words, one creates a new type of society, when not working, in which one can feel more at home. It need not have the slightest connection with what his ordinary occupation is. It is an escape, and not necessarily an unhealthy one." He smiled and added, "Myself, I collect stamps. I am an active member of the American Society of Philatelists."

Grant shook his head, "I don't know what he did outside working hours. I doubt that he did anything like what you've mentioned."

"Um-m-m. Well, that would be sad. Relaxation and enjoyment are wherever you find them; but you must find them somewhere, no?"

"Have you spoken to Dr. Ralson, yet?"

"About his problem? No."

"Aren't you going to?"

"Oh, yes. But he has been here only a week. One must give him

64

a chance to recover. He was in a highly excited state when he first came here. It was almost a delirium. Let him rest and become accustomed to the new environment. I will question him, then."

"Will you be able to get him back to work?"

Blaustein smiled, "How should I know? I don't even know what his sickness is?"

"Couldn't you at least get rid of the worst of it; this suicidal obsession of his, and take care of the rest of the cure while he's at work."

"Perhaps. I couldn't even venture an opinion so far without several interviews."

"How long do you suppose it will take?"

"In these matters, Dr. Grant, nobody can say."

Grant brought his hands together in a sharp slap, "Do what seems best then. But this is more important than you know."

"Perhaps you may be able to help me, Dr. Grant."

"How?"

"Can you get me certain information which may be classified as top secret."

"What kind of information?"

"I would like to know the suicide rate, since 1945, among nuclear scientists. Also, how many have left their jobs to go into other types of scientific work, or to leave science altogether."

"Is this in connection with Ralson?"

"Don't you think it might be an occupational disease, this terrible unhappiness of his?"

"Well—A good many have left their jobs, naturally."

"Why naturally, Dr. Grant?"

"You must know how it is, Dr. Blaustein. The atmosphere in modern atomic research is one of great pressure and red tape. You work with the Government; you work with military men. You can't talk about your work; you have to be careful what you say. Naturally, if you get a chance at a job in a University, where you can fix your own hours, do your own work, write papers that don't have to be submitted to the A.E.C., attend conventions that aren't held behind locked doors, you take it."

"And abandon your field of specialty forever."

"There are always nonmilitary applications. Of course, there was one man who did leave for another reason. He told me once he couldn't sleep nights. He said he'd hear one hundred thousand screams coming from Hiroshima, when he put the lights out. The last I heard of him he was a clerk in a haberdashery."

"And do you ever hear a few screams yourself?"

Grant nodded, "It isn't a nice feeling to know that even a little of the responsibility of atomic destruction might be your own."

"How did Ralson feel?"

"He never spoke of anything like that."

"In other words, if he felt it, he never even had the safety-valve effect of letting off steam to the rest of you."

"I guess he hadn't."

"Yet nuclear research must be done, no?"

"I'll say."

"What would you do, Dr. Grant, if you felt you *had* to do something that you *couldn't* do."

Grant shrugged, "I don't know."

"Some people kill themselves."

"You mean that's what has Ralson down."

"I don't know. I do not know. I will speak to Dr. Ralson this evening. I can promise nothing, of course, but I will let you know whatever I can."

Grant rose, "Thanks, doctor. I'll try to get the information you want."

Elwood Ralson's appearance had improved in the week he had been at Dr. Blaustein's sanitarium. His face had filled out and some of the restlessness had gone out of him. He was tieless and beltless. His shoes were without laces.

Blaustein said, "How do you feel, Dr. Ralson?"

"Rested."

"You have been treated well?"

"No complaints, doctor."

Blaustein's hand fumbled for the letter-opener with which it was his habit to play during moments of abstraction, but his fingers met nothing. It had been put away, of course, with anything else possessing a sharp edge. There was nothing on his desk, now, but papers.

He said, "Sit down, Dr. Ralson. How do your symptons progress?"

"You mean, do I have what you would call a suicidal impulse? Yes. It gets worse or better, depending on my thoughts, I think. But it's always with me. There is nothing you can do to help."

"Perhaps you are right. There are often things I cannot help. But I would like to know as much as I can about you. You are an important man—"

Ralson snorted.

"You do not consider that to be so?" asked Blaustein.

"No, I don't. There are no important men, any more than there are important individual bacteria."

"I don't understand."

"I don't expect you to."

"And yet it seems to me that behind your statement there must have been much thought. It would certainly be of the greatest interest to have you tell me some of this thought."

For the first time, Ralson smiled. It was not a pleasant smile. His nostrils were white. He said, "It is amusing to watch you, doctor. You go about your business so conscientiously. You must listen to me, mustn't you, with just that air of phony interest and unctuous sympathy. I can tell you the most ridiculous things and still be sure of an audience, can't I?"

"Don't you think my interest can be real, even granted that it is professional, too?"

"No, I don't."

"Why not?"

"I'm not interested in discussing it."

"Would you rather return to your room?"

"If you don't mind. No!" His voice had suddenly suffused with fury as he stood up, then almost immediately sat down again, "Why shouldn't I use you? I don't like to talk to people. They're stupid. They don't see things. They stare at the obvious for hours and it means nothing to them. If I spoke to them, they wouldn't understand; they'd lose patience; they'd laugh. Whereas you must listen. It's your job. You can't interrupt to tell me I'm mad, even though you may think so."

"I'd be glad to listen to whatever you would like to tell me."

Ralson drew a deep breath, "I've known something for a year now, that very few people know. Maybe it's something no *live* person knows. Do you know that human cultural advances come in spurts. Over a space of two generations in a city containing thirty thousand free men, enough literary and artistic genius of the first rank arose to supply a nation of millions for a century under ordinary circumstances. I'm referring to the Athens of Pericles.

"There are other examples. There is the Florence of the Medicis, the England of Elizabeth, the Spain of the Cordovan Emirs. There was the spasm of social reformers among the Israelites of the Eighth and Seventh centuries before Christ. Do you know what I mean?"

Blaustein nodded, "I see that history is a subject that interests you."

"Why not? I suppose there's nothing that says I must restrict myself to nuclear cross-sections and wave mechanics."

"Nothing at all. Please proceed."

"At first, I thought I could learn more of the true inwardness of historical cycles by consulting a specialist. I had some conferences with a professional historian. A waste of time!"

"What was his name; this professional historian?"

"Does it matter?"

"Perhaps not, if you would rather consider it confidential. What did he tell you?"

"He said I was wrong; that history only appeared to go in spasms. He said that after closer studies the great civilizations of Egypt and Sumeria did not arise suddenly or out of nothing, but upon the basis of a long-developing subcivilization that was already sophisticated in its arts. He said that Periclean Athens was built upon a pre-Periclean Athens of lower accomplishments, without which the age of Pericles could not have been.

"I asked him why was there not a post-Periclean Athens of higher accomplishments still, and he told me that Athens was ruined by a plague and by the long war with Sparta. I asked about other cultural spurts and each time it was a war that ended it, or, in some cases, even accompanied it. He was like all the rest. The truth was there; he had only to bend and pick it up; but he didn't."

Ralson stared at the floor, and said in a tired voice, "They come to me in the laboratory sometimes, doctor. They say, 'How the devil are we going to get rid of the such-and-such effect that is ruining all our measurements, Ralson?' They show me the instruments and the wiring diagrams and I say, 'It's staring at you. Why don't you do so-and-so? A child could tell you that." Then I walk away because I can't endure the slow puzzling of their stupid faces. Later, they come to me again and say, 'It worked, Ralson. How did you figure it out?' I can't explain to them, doctor; it would be like explaining that water is wet. And I couldn't explain to the historian. And I can't explain to you. It's a waste of time."

"Would you like to go back to your room?"

"Yes."

Blaustein sat and wondered for many minutes after Ralson had been escorted out of his office. His fingers found their way automatically into the upper right drawer of his desk and lifted out the letter-opener. He twiddled it in his fingers.

Finally, he lifted the telephone, and dialed the unlisted number he had been given.

He said, "This is Blaustein. There is a professional historian who was consulted by Dr. Ralson some time in the past, probably a bit over a year ago. I don't know his name. I don't even know if he was connected with a University. If you could find him; I would like to see him."

Thaddeus Milton, Ph.D. blinked thoughtfully at Blaustein and brushed his hand through his iron-gray hair. He said, "They came to me and I said that I indeed met this man. However, I have had very little connection with him. None, in fact, beyond a few conversations of a professional nature."

"How did he come to you?"

"He wrote me a letter; why me, rather than someone else, I do not know. A series of articles written by myself had appeared in one of the semilearned journals of semipopular appeal about that time It may have attracted his attention."

"I see. With what general topic were the articles concerned?"

"They were a consideration of the validity of the cyclic approach to history. That is, whether one can really say that a particular civilization must follow the laws of growth and decline in any matter analogous to those involving individuals."

"I have read Toynbee, Dr. Milton."

"Well, then, you know what I mean."

Blaustein said, "And when Dr. Ralson consulted you, was it with reference to this cyclic approach to history?"

"U-m-m-m. In a way, I suppose. Of course, the man is not an historian and some of his notions about cultural trends are rather dramatic and . . . what shall I say . . . tabloidish. Pardon me, doctor, if I ask a question which may be improper. Is Dr. Ralson one of your patients. ?"

"Dr. Ralson is not well and is in my care. This, and all else we say here is confidential, of course."

"Quite. I understand that. However, your answer explains something to me. Some of his ideas almost verged on the irrational. He was always worried, it seemed to me, about the connection between what he called 'cultural spurts' and calamities of one sort or another. Now such connections have been noted frequently. The time of a nation's greatest vitality may come at a time of great national insecurity. The Netherlands is a good case in point. Its great artists, statesmen and explorers belong to the early Seventeenth Century at the time when she was locked in a death struggle with the greatest European power of the time, Spain. When at the point of destruction at home, she was building an empire in the Far East and had secured footholds on the northern coast of South America, the southern tip of Africa, and the Hudson Valley of North America. Her fleets fought England to a standstill. And then, once her political safety was assured, she declined.

"Well, as I say, that is not unusual. Groups, like individuals, will rise to strange heights in answer to a challenge, and vegetate in the absence of a challenge. Where Dr. Ralson left the paths of sanity, however, was in insisting that such a view amounted to confusing cause and effect. He declared that it was not times of war and danger that stimulated 'cultural spurts,' but rather vice versa. He claimed that each time a group of men showed too much vitality and ability, a war became necessary to destroy the posibility of their further development."

"I see," said Blaustein.

"I rather laughed at him, I am afraid. It may be that that was why he did not keep the last appointment we made. Just toward the end of the last conference he asked me, in the most intense fashion imaginable, whether I did not think it queer that such an improbable species as Man was dominant on Earth, when all he had in his favor was intelligence. There I laughed aloud. Perhaps I should not have, poor fellow."

"It was a natural reaction," said Blaustein, "but I must take no more of your time. You have been most helpful."

They shook hands, and Thaddeus Milton took his leave.

"Well," said Darrity, "there are your figures on the recent suicides among scientific personnel. Get any deductions out of it?"

"I should be asking you that," said Blaustein, gently. "The F.B.I. must have investigated thoroughly."

"You can bet the national debt on that. They *are* suicides. There's no mistake about it. There have been people checking on it in another department. The rate is about four times above normal, taking age, social status, economic class into consideration."

"What about British scientists?"

"Just about the same."

"And the Soviet Union?"

"Who can tell?" The investigator leaned forward, "Doc, you don't think the Soviets have some sort of ray that can make people want to commit suicide, do you? It's sort of suspicious that men in atomic research are the only ones affected."

"Is it? Perhaps not. Nuclear physicists may have peculiar strains imposed upon them. It is difficult to tell without thorough study."

"You mean complexes might be coming through," asked Darrity, warily.

70

Blaustein made a face, "Psychiatry is becoming too popular. Everybody talks of complexes and neuroses and psychoses and compulsions and what-not. One man's guilt complex is another man's good night's sleep. If I could talk to each one of the men who committed suicide, maybe I could know something."

"You're talking to Ralson."

"Yes, I'm talking to Ralson."

"Has *he* got a guilt complex?"

"Not particularly. He has a background out of which it would not surprise me if he obtained a morbid concern with death. When he was twelve he saw his mother die under the wheels of an automobile. His father died slowly of cancer. Yet the effect of that on his present troubles is not clear."

Darrity picked up his hat, "Well, I wish you would get a move on, doc. There's something big on, bigger than the H-Bomb. I don't know how anything *can* be bigger than that, but it is."

Ralson insisted on standing, "I had a bad night last night, doctor."

"I hope," said Blaustein, "these conferences are not disturbing you."

"Well, maybe they are. It has me thinking on the subject again. It also makes things bad, when I do that. How do you imagine it feels being part of a bacterial culture, doctor?"

"I had never thought of that. To a bacterium, it probably feels quite normal."

Ralson did not hear. He said slowly, "A culture in which intelligence is being studied. We study all sorts of things as far as their genetic relationships are concerned. We take fruit flies and cross red eyes with white eyes to see what happens. We don't care anything about red eyes and white eyes, but we try to gather from them certain basic genetic principles. You see what I mean?"

"Certainly."

"Even in humans, we can follow various physical characteristics. There is the Hapsburg lip, and the hemophilia that started with Queen Victoria and cropped up in her descendants among the Spanish and Russian royal families. We can even follow feeble-mindedness in the Jukes and Kallikaks. You learn about it in high-school biology. But you can't breed human beings the way you do fruit flies. Humans live too long. It would take centuries to draw conclusions. It's a pity we don't have a special race of men that reproduce at weekly intervals, eh?"

He waited for an answer, but Blaustein only smiled.

71

Ralson said, "Only that's exactly what we would be for another group of beings whose life span might be thousands of years. To them, we would reproduce rapidly enough. We would be short-lived creatures and they could study the genetics of such things as musical aptitude, scientific intelligence and so on. Not that those things would interest them as such, any more than the white eyes of the fruit fly interest us as white eyes."

"This is a very interesting notion," said Blaustein.

"It is not simply a notion. It is true. To me, it is obvious, and I don't care how it seems to you. Look around you. Look at the planet, Earth. What kind of a ridiculous animal are we to be lords of the world after the dinosaurs had failed. Sure, we're intelligent, but what's intelligence? We think it is important because we have it. If the Tyranosaurus could have picked out the one quality that he thought would ensure species domination, it would be size and strength. And he would make a better case for it. He lasted longer than we're likely to.

"Intelligence in itself isn't much as far as survival values are concerned. The elephant makes out very poorly indeed when compared to the sparrow even though he is much more intelligent. The dog does well, under man's protection, but not as well as the housefly against whom every human hand is raised. Or take the primates as a group. The small ones cower before their enemies; the large ones have always been remarkably unsuccessful in doing more than barely holding their own. The baboons do their best and that is because of their canines, not their brains."

A light film of perspiration covered Ralson's forehead, "And one can see that man has been tailored, made to careful specifications for those things that study us. Generally, the primate is short-lived. Naturally, the larger ones live longer, which is a fairly general rule in animal life. Yet the human being has a life span twice as long as any of the other great apes; considerably longer even than the gorilla that outweighs him. We mature later. It's as though we've been carefully bred to live a little longer so that our life cycle might be more of a convenient length."

He jumped to his feet, shaking his fists above his head, "A thousand years is a day—"

Blaustein punched a button hastily.

For a moment, Ralson struggled against the white-coated orderly who entered, and then he allowed himself to be led away.

Blaustein looked after him, shook his head, and picked up the telephone.

72

He got Darrity, "Inspector, you may as well know that this may take a long time."

He listened and shook his head, "I know. I don't minimize the urgency."

The voice in the receiver was tinny and harsh, "Doctor, you *are* minimizing it. I'll send Dr. Grant to you. He'll explain the situation to you."

Dr. Grant asked how Ralson was, then asked somewhat wistfully if he could see him. Blaustein shook his head gently.

Grant said, "I've been directed to explain the current situation in atomic research to you."

"So that I will understand, no?"

"I hope so. It's a measure of desperation. I'll have to remind you—"

"Not to breathe a word of it. Yes I know. This insecurity on the part of you people is a very bad symptom. You must know these things cannot be hidden."

"You live with secrecy. It's contagious."

"Exactly. What is the current secret?"

"There is . . . or, at least, there might be a defense against the atomic bomb."

"And that is a secret? It would be better it should be shouted to all the people of the world instantly."

"For heaven's sake, no. Listen to me, Dr. Blaustein. It's only on paper so far. It's at the E equals mc square stage, almost. It may not be practical. It would be bad to raise hopes we would have to disappoint. On the other hand, if it were known that we *almost* had a defense, there *might be* a desire to start and win a war before the defense were completely developed."

"That I don't believe. Wars are not started; they happen. But, nevertheless, I distract you. What is the nature of this defense, or have you told me as much as you dare?"

"No, I can go as far as I like; as far as is necessary to convince you we have to have Ralson—and fast!"

"Well, then tell me, and I, too, will know the secrets. I'll feel like a member of the cabinet."

"You'll know more than most. Look, Dr. Blaustein, let me explain it in lay language. So far, military advances have been made fairly equally in both offensive and defensive weapons. Once before there seemed to be a definite and permanent tipping of all warfare in the direction of the offense, and that was with the invention of gunpowder. But the defense caught up. The medieval

73

man-in-armor-on-horse became the modern man-in-tank-on-treads, and the stone castle became the concrete pillbox. The same thing you see, except that everything has been boosted several orders of magnitude."

"Very good. You make it clear. But with the atomic bomb comes more orders of magnitude, no? You must go past concrete and steel for protection."

"Right. Only we can't just make thicker and thicker walls. We've run out of materials that are strong enough. So we must abandon materials altogether. If the atom attacks, we must let the atom defend. We will use energy itself; a force field."

"And what," asked Dr. Blaustein, gently, "is a force field?"

"I wish I could tell you. Right now, it's an equation on paper. Energy can be so channeled as to create a wall of matterless inertia, theoretically. In practice, we don't know how to do it."

"It would be a wall you could not go through, is that it? Even for atoms?"

"Even for atom bombs. The only limit on its strength would be the amount of energy we could pour into it. It could even theoretically be made to be impermeable to radiation. It would bounce off the gamma rays. What we're dreaming of is a screen that would be in permanent place about cities; at minimum strength, using practically no energy. It could then be triggered to maximum intensity in a fraction of a millisecond at the impingement of short-wave radiation; say the amount radiating from a mass of plutonium large enough to be an atomic war head. All this is theoretically possible.

"And why must you have Ralson?"

"Because he is the only one who can reduce it to practice, if it can be made practical at all, quickly enough. Every minute counts these days. You know what the international situation is like. Atomic defense *must* arrive before atomic war."

"You are so sure of Ralson?"

"I am as sure of him as I can be of anything. The man is amazing, Dr. Blaustein. He is always right. Nobody in the field knows how he does it."

"A sort of intuition, no?" The psychiatrist looked disturbed, "A kind of reasoning that goes beyond ordinary human capacities. Is that it?"

"I make no pretense of knowing what it is."

"Let me speak to him once more, then. I will let you know."

"Good." Grant rose to leave; then, as if in afterthought, he said, "I might say, doctor, that if you don't do something, the

Commission plans to take Dr. Ralson out of your hands."

"And try another psychiatrist? If they wish to do that, of course, I will not stand in their way. It is my opinion, however, that no reputable practitioner will pretend there is a rapid cure."

"We may not intend further mental treatment. He may simply be returned to work."

"That, Dr. Grant, I will fight. You will get nothing out of him. It will be his death."

"We get nothing out of him anyway."

"This way there is at least a chance, no?"

"I hope so. And by the way, please don't mention the fact that I said anything about taking Ralson away."

"I will not, and I thank you for the warning. Good-by, Dr. Grant."

"I made a fool of myself last time, didn't I, doctor?" said Ralson. He was frowning.

"You mean you don't believe what you said then?"

"*I do!*" Ralson's slight form trembled with the intensity of his affirmation.

He rushed to the window, and Blaustein swiveled in his chair to keep him in view. There were bars in the window. He couldn't jump. The glass was unbreakable.

Twilight was ending, and the stars were beginning to come out. Ralson stared at them in fascination, then he turned to Blaustein and flung a finger outward, "Every single one of them is an incubator. They maintain temperatures at the desired point. Different experiments; different temperatures. And the planets that circle them are just huge cultures, containing different nutrient mixtures and different life forms. The experimenters are economical, too—whatever and whoever they are. They've cultured many types of life forms in this particular test tube. Dinosaurs in a moist, tropical age and ourselves among the glaciers. They turn the sun up and down and we try to work out the physics of it. Physics!" He drew his lips back in a snarl.

"Surely," said Dr. Blaustein, "it is not possible that the sun can be turned up and down at will."

"Why not? It's just like a heating element in an oven. You think bacteria know what it is that works the heat that reaches them? Who knows? Maybe they evolve theories, too. Maybe they have their cosmogonies about cosmic catastrophes, in which clashing light-bulbs create strings of Petri dishes. Maybe they think there must be some beneficent creator that supplies them with food and warmth and says to them, 'Be fruitful and multiply!'

"We breed like them, not knowing why. We obey the so-called laws of Nature which are only our interpretation of the not-understood forces imposed upon us.

"And now they've got the biggest experiment of any yet on their hands. It's been going on for two hundred years. They decided to develop a strain for mechanical aptitude in England in the seventeen hundreds, I imagine. We call it the Industrial Revolution. It began with steam, went on to electricity, then atoms. It was an interesting experiment, but they took their chances on letting it spread. Which is why they'll have to be very drastic indeed in ending it."

Blaustein said, "And how would they plan to end it? Do you have an idea about that?"

"You ask *me* how they plan to end it. You can look about the world today and still ask what is likely to bring our technological age to an end. All the Earth fears an atomic war and would do anything to avoid it; yet all the Earth fears that an atomic war is inevitable."

"In other words, the experimenters will arrange an atom war whether we want it or not, to kill off the technological era we are in, and to start fresh. That is it, no?"

"Yes. It's logical. When we sterilize an instrument, do the germs know where the killing heat comes from? Or what has brought it about? There is some way the experimenters can raise the heat of our emotions; some way they can handle us that passes our understanding."

"Tell me," said Blaustein, "is that why you want to die? Because you think the destruction of civilization is coming and can't be stopped?"

Ralson said, "I *don't* want to die. It's just that I must." His eyes were tortured, "Doctor, if you had a culture of germs that were highly dangerous and that you had to keep under absolute control, might you not have an agar medium impregnated with, say, penicillin, in a circle at a certain distance from the center of inoculation? Any germs spreading out too far from that center would die. You would have nothing against the particular germs who were killed; you might not even know that any germs had spread that far in the first place. It would be purely automatic.

"Doctor, there is a penicillin ring about our intellects. When we stray too far; when we penetrate the true meaning of our own
76

existence, we have reached into the penicillin and we must die. It works slowly—but it's hard to stay alive."

He smiled briefly and sadly. Then he said, "May I go back to my room now, doctor?"

Dr. Blaustein went to Ralson's room about noon the next day. It was a small room and featureless. The walls were gray with padding. Two small windows were high up and could not be reached. The mattress lay directly on the padded floor. There was nothing of metal in the room; nothing that could be utilized in tearing life from body. Even Ralson's nails were clipped short.

Ralson sat up, "Hello!"

"Hello, Dr. Ralson. May I speak to you?"

"Here? There isn't any seat I can offer you."

"It is all right. I'll stand. I have a sitting job and it is good for my sitting-down place that I should stand sometimes. Dr. Ralson I have thought all night of what you told me yesterday and in the days before."

"And now you are going to apply treatment to rid me of what you think are delusions."

"No. It is just that I wish to ask questions and perhaps to point out some consequences of your theories which . . . you will forgive me? . . . you may not have thought of."

"Oh?"

"You see, Dr. Ralson, since you have explained your theories, I, too, know what you know. Yet I have no feeling about suicide."

"Belief is more than something intellectual, doctor. You'd have to believe this with all your insides, which you don't"

"Do you not think perhaps it is rather a phenomenon of adaptation?"

"How do you mean?"

"You are not really a biologist, Dr. Ralson. And although you are very brilliant indeed in physics, you do not think of everything with respect to these bacterial cultures you use as analogies. You know that it is possible to breed bacterial strains that are resistant to penicillin or to almost any bacterial poison."

"Well?"

"The experimenters who breed us have been working with humanity for many generations, no? And this particular strain which they have been culturing for two centuries shows no signs of drying out spontaneously. Rather, it is a vigorous strain and a very infective one. Older high-culture strains were confined to single cities or to small areas and lasted only a generation or two.

77

This one is spreading throughout the world. It is a *very* infective strain. Do you not think it may have developed penicillin immunity? In other words, the methods the experimenters use to wipe out the culture may not work too well any more, no?"

Ralson shook his head, "It's working on me."

"You are perhaps nonresistant. Or you have stumbled into a very high concentration of penicillin indeed. Consider all the people who have been trying to outlaw atomic warfare and to establish some form of world government and lasting peace. The effort has risen in recent years, without too awful results."

"It isn't stopping the atomic war that's coming."

"No, but maybe only a little more effort is all that is required. The peace advocates do not kill themselves. More and more humans are immune to the experimenters. Do you know what they are doing in the laboratory?"

"I don't want to know."

"You *must* know. They are trying to invent a force field that will stop the atom bomb. Dr. Ralson, if I am culturing a virulent and pathological bacterium; then, even with all precautions, it may sometimes happen that I will start a plague. We may be bacteria to them, but we are dangerous to them, also, or they wouldn't wipe us out so carefully after each experiment.

"They are not quick, no? To them a thousand years is as a day, no? By the time they realize we are out of the culture, past the penicillin, it will be too late for them to stop us. They have brought us to the atom, and if we can only prevent ourselves from using it upon one another, we may turn out to be too much even for the experimenters."

Ralson rose to his feet. Small though he was, he was an inch and a half taller than Blaustein. "They are really working on a force field?"

"They are trying to. But they need you."

"No, I can't."

"They must have you in order that you might see what is so obvious to you. It is not obvious to them. Remember, it is your help, or else—defeat of man by the experimenters."

Ralson took a few rapid steps away, staring into the blank, padded wall. He muttered, "But there must be that defeat. If they build a force field, it will mean death for all of them before it can be completed."

"Some or all of them may be immune, no? And in any case, it will be death for them anyhow. They are trying."

Ralson said, "I'll try to help them."

78

"Do you still want to kill yourself?"

"Yes."

"But you'll try not to, no?"

"I'll *try* not to, doctor." His lip quivered. "I'll have to be watched."

Blaustein climbed the stairs and presented his pass to the guard in the lobby. He had already been inspected at the outer gate, but he, his pass, and its signature were now scrutinized once again. After a moment, the guard retired to his little cubby and made a phone call. The answer satisfied him. Blaustein took a seat and, in half a minute, was up again, shaking hands with Dr. Grant.

"The President of the United States would have trouble getting in here, no?" said Blaustein.

The lanky physicist smiled. "You're right, if he came without warning."

They took an elevator which traveled twelve floors. The office to which Grant led the way had windows in three directions. It was soundproofed and air-conditioned. Its walnut furniture was in a state of high polish.

Blaustein said, "My goodness. It is like the office of the chairman of a board of directors. Science is becoming big business."

Grant looked embarrassed, "Yes, I know, but government money flows easily and it is difficult to persuade a congressman that your work is important unless he can see, smell, and touch the surface shine."

Blaustein sat down and felt the upholstered seat give way slowly. He said, "Dr. Elwood Ralson has agreed to return to work."

"Wonderful. I was hoping you would say that. I was hoping that that was why you wanted to see me." As though inspired by the news, Grant offered the psychiatrist a cigar, which was refused.

"However," said Blaustein, "he remains a very sick man. He will have to be treated carefully and with insight."

"Of course. Naturally."

"It's not quite as simple as you may think. I want to tell you something of Ralson's problems, so that you will really understand how delicate the situation is."

He went on talking and Grant listened first in concern, and then in astonishment. "But then the man is out of his head, Dr. Blaustein. He'll be of no use to us. He's crazy."

Blaustein shrugged, "It depends on how you define 'crazy.' It's

79

a bad word; don't use it. He has delusions, certainly. Whether they will affect his peculiar talents one cannot know."

"But surely no sane man could possibly—"

"Please. Please. Let us not launch into long discussions on psychiatric definitions of sanity and so on. The man has delusions and, ordinarily, I would dismiss them from all consideration. It is just that I have been given to understand that the man's particular ability lies in his manner of proceeding to the solution of a problem by what seems to be outside ordinary reason. That is so, no?"

"Yes. That *must* be admitted."

"And other scientists here?"

"How can you and I judge then as to the worth of one of his conclusions. Let me ask you, do *you* have suicidal impulses lately?"

"I don't think so."

"No, of course not."

"I would suggest, however, that while research on the force field proceeds, the scientists concerned be watched here and at home. It might even be a good enough idea they that should not go home. Offices like these could be arranged to be a small dormitory—"

"Sleep at work. You would never get them to agree."

"Oh, yes. If you do not tell them the real reason but say it is for security purposes, they will agree. 'Security purposes' is a wonderful phrase these days, no? Ralson must be watched more than any one."

"Of course."

"But all this is minor. It is something to be done to satisfy my conscience in case Ralson's theories are correct. Actually, I don't believe them. They *are* delusions, but once that is granted, it is necessary to ask what the causes of those delusions are. What is it in Ralson's mind, in his background, in his life that makes it so necessary for him to have these particular delusions? One cannot answer that simply. It may well take years of constant psychoanalysis to discover the answer. And until the answer is discovered he will not be cured.

"But, meanwhile, we can perhaps make intelligent guesses. He has had an unhappy childhood, which, in one way or another, has brought him face to face with death in very unpleasant fashion. In addition, he has never been able to form associations with other children, or, as he grew older, with other men. He was always impatient with their slower forms of reasoning. Whatever difference there is between his mind and that of others, it has built

80

a wall between them and society as strong as the force field you are trying to design. For similar reasons, he has been unable to enjoy a normal sex life. He has never married; he has had no sweethearts.

"It is easy to see that he could easily compensate to himself for this failure to be accepted by his social milieu by taking refuge in the thought that other human beings are inferior to himself. Which is, of course, true, as far as mentality is concerned. There are, of course, many, many facets to the human personality and in not all of them is he superior. No one is. Others, then, who are more prone to see merely what is inferior, just as he himself is, would not accept his affected preeminence of position. They would think him queer, even laughable, which would make it even more important to Ralson to prove how miserable and inferior the human species was. How could he better do that than to show that mankind was simply a form of bacteria to other superior creatures which experiment upon them. And then his impulses to suicide would be a wild desire to break away completely from being a man at all; to stop this identification with the miserable species he has created in his mind. You see?"

Grant nodded, "Poor guy."

"Yes, it is a pity. Had he been properly taken care of in childhood—Well, it is best for Dr. Grant that he have no contact with any of the other men here. He is too sick to be trusted with them. You, yourself, must arrange to be the only man who will see him or speak to him. Dr. Ralson has agreed to that. He apparently thinks you are not so stupid as some of the others."

Grant smiled faintly, "That is agreeable to me."

"You will, of course, be careful. I would not discuss anything with him but his work. If he should volunteer information about his theories, which I doubt, confine yourself to something non-committal, and leave. And at all times, keep away anything that is sharp and pointed. Do not let him reach a window. Try to have his hands kept in view. You understand. I leave my patient in your care, Dr. Grant."

"I will do my best, Dr. Blaustein."

For two months, Ralson lived in a corner of Grant's office, and Grant lived with him. Gridwork had been built up before the windows; wooden furniture was removed and upholstered sofas brought in. Ralson did his thinking on the couch and his calculating on a desk pad atop a hassock.

The "Do Not Enter" was a permanent fixture outside the office.

Meals were left outside. The adjoining men's room was marked off for private use and the door between it and the office removed. Grant switched to an electric razor. He made certain that Ralson took sleeping pills each night and waited till the other slept before sleeping himself.

And always reports were brought to Ralson. He read them while Grant watched and tried to seem not to watch.

Then Ralson would let them drop and stare at the ceiling, with one hand shading his eyes.

"Anything?" asked Grant.

Ralson shook his head from side to side.

Grant said, "Look, I'll clear the building during the swing shift. It's important that you see some of the experimental jigs we've been setting up."

They did so, wandering through the lighted, empty buildings like drifting ghosts, hand in hand. Always hand in hand. Grant's grip was tight. But after each trip, Ralson would still shake his head from side to side.

Half a dozen times he would begin writing; each time there would be a few scrawls, and then he would kick the hassock over on its side.

Until, finally, he began writing once again and covered half a page rapidly. Automatically, Grant approached. Ralson looked up, covering the sheet of paper with a trembling hand.

He said, "Call Blaustein."

"What?"

"I said, call Blaustein. Get him here. Now!"

Grant moved to the telephone.

Ralson was writing rapidly now, stopping only to brush wildly at his forehead with the back of a hand. It came away wet.

He looked up and his voice was cracked, "Is he coming?"

Grant looked worried, "He isn't at his office."

"Get him at his home. Get him wherever he is. *Use* that telephone. Don't play with it."

Grant used it; and Ralson pulled another sheet toward himself.

Five minutes later, Grant said, "He's coming. What's wrong? You're looking sick."

Ralson could only speak thickly, "No time—Can't talk—"

He was writing, scribbling, scrawling, shakily diagramming. It was as though he were driving his hands, fighting it.

"Dictate!" urged Grant. "I'll write."

Ralson shook him off. His words were unintelligible. He held

82

his right wrist with his other hand, shoving it as though it were a piece of wood, and then collapsed over the papers.

Grant edged them out from under and laid Ralson down on the couch. He hovered over him restlessly until Blaustein arrived.

Blaustein took one look, "What happened?"

Grant said, "I think he's alive," but by that time Blaustein had verified that for himself, and Grant told him what had happened.

Blaustein used a hypodermic and they waited. Ralson's eyes were blank when they opened. He moaned.

Blaustein leaned close, "Ralson."

Ralson's hands reached out blindly and clutched at the psychiatrist, "Doc. Take me back."

"I will. Now. It is that you have the force field worked out, no?"

"It's on the papers. Grant, it's on the papers."

Grant had them and was leafing through them dubiously. Ralson said, weakly, "It's not *all* there. It's all I can write. You'll *have* to make it out of that. Take me back, doc!"

"Wait," said Grant. He whispered urgently to Blaustein, "Can't you leave him here till we test this thing? I can't make out what most of this is. The writing is illegible. Ask him what makes him think this will work."

"Ask *him*?" said Blaustein, gently. "Isn't he the one who always knows?"

"Ask me, anyway," said Ralson, overhearing from where he lay on the couch. His eyes were suddenly wide and blazing.

They turned to him.

He said, "*They* don't want a force field. *They!* The experimenters! As long as I had no true grasp, things remained as they were. But I hadn't followed up that thought—*that* thought which is there in the papers—I hadn't followed it up for thirty seconds before I felt ... I felt—Doctor—"

Blaustein said, "What is it?"

Ralson was whispering again, "I'm deeper in the penicillin. I could feel myself plunging in and in, the further I went with that. I've never been in ... so deep. That's how I knew I was right. Take me away."

Blaustein straightened, "I'll have to take him away, Grant. There's no alternative. If you can make out what he's written, that's it. If you can't make it out, I can't help you. That man can do no more work in his field without dying, do you understand?"

"But," said Grant, "he's dying of something imaginary."

"All right. Say that he is. But he will be really dead just the same, no?"

Ralson was unconscious again and heard nothing of this. Grant looked at him somberly, then said, "Well, take him away, then."

Ten of the top men at the Institute watched glumly as slide after slide filled the illuminated screen. Grant faced them, expression hard and frowning.

He said, "I think the idea is simple enough. You're mathematicians and you're engineers. The scrawl may seem illegible, but it was done with meaning behind it. That meaning must somehow remain in the writing, distorted though it is. The first page is clear enough. It should be a good lead. Each one of you will look at every page over and over again. You're going to put down every possible version of each page as it seems it might be. You will work independently. I want no consultations."

One of them said, "How do you know it means *anything*, Grant?"

"Because those are Ralson's notes."

"*Ralson!* I thought he was—"

"You thought he was sick," said Grant. He had to shout over the rising hum of conversation. "I know. He is. That's the writing of a man who was nearly dead. It's all we'll ever get from Ralson, any more. Somewhere in that scrawl is the answer to the force field problem. If we can't find it, we may have to spend ten years looking for it elsewhere."

They bent to their work. The night passed. Two nights passed. Three nights—

Grant looked at the results. He shook his head, "I'll take your word for it that it is all self-consistent. I can't say I understand it."

Lowe, who, in the absence of Ralson, would readily have been rated the best nuclear engineer in the Institute, shrugged, "It's not exactly clear to me. If it works, he hasn't explained why."

"He had no time to explain. Can you build a generator as he describes it?"

"I could try."

"Would you look at all the other versions of the pages?"

"The others are definitely not self-consistent."

"Would you double check?"

"Sure."

"And you could start construction anyway?"

"I'll get the shop started. But I tell you frankly that I'm pessimistic."

"I know. So am I."

84

The thing grew. Hal Ross, Senior Mechanic, was put in charge of the actual construction, and he stopped sleeping. At any hour of the day or night, he could be found at it, scratching his bald head.

He asked questions only once, "What is it, Dr. Lowe? Never saw anything like it? What's it supposed to do?"

Lowe said, "You know where you are, Ross. You know we don't ask questions here. Don't ask again."

Ross did not ask again. He was known to dislike the structure that was being built. He called it ugly and unnatural. But he stayed at it.

Blaustein called one day.

Grant said, "How's Ralson?"

"Not good. He wants to attend the testing of the Field Projector he designed."

Grant hesitated, "I suppose we should. It's his after all."

"I would have to come with him."

Grant looked unhappier, "It might be dangerous, you know. Even in a pilot test, we'd be playing with tremendous energies."

Blaustein said, "No more dangerous for us than for you."

"Very well. The list of observers will have to be cleared through the Commission and the F.B.I., but I'll put you in."

Blaustein looked about him. The Field Projector squatted in the very center of the huge testing laboratory, but all else had been cleared. There was no visible connection with the plutonium pile which served as energy-source, but from what the psychiatrist heard in scraps about him—he knew better than to ask Ralson—the connection was from beneath.

At first, the observers had circled the machine, talking in incomprehensibles, but they were drifting away now. The gallery was filling up. There were at least three men in generals' uniforms on the other side, and a real coterie of lower scale military. Blaustein chose an unoccupied portion of the railing; for Ralson's sake, most of all.

He said, "Do you still think you would like to stay?"

It was warm enough within the laboratory, but Ralson was in his coat, with his collar turned up. It made little difference, Blaustein felt. He doubted that any of Ralson's former acquaintances would now recognise him.

Ralson said, "I'll stay."

Blaustein was pleased. He wanted to see the test. He turned again at a new voice.

"Hello, Dr. Blaustein."

For a minute, Blaustein did not place him, then he said, "Ah, Inspector Darrity. What are you doing here?"

"Just what you would suppose." He indicated the watchers. "There isn't any way you can weed them out so that you can be sure there won't be any mistakes. I once stood as near to Klaus Fuchs as I am standing to you." He tossed his pocketknife into the air and retrieved it with a dexterous motion.

"Ah, yes, Where shall one find perfect security? What man can trust even his own unconsciousness? And you will now stand near to me, no?"

"Might as well." Darrity smiled, "You were very anxious to get in here, weren't you?"

"Not for myself, inspector. And would you put away the knife, please."

Darrity turned in surprise in the direction of Blaustein's gentle head-gesture. He put his knife away and looked at Blaustein's companion for the second time. He whistled softly.

He said, "Hello, Dr. Ralson."

Ralson croaked, "Hello."

Blaustein was not surprised at Darrity's reaction. Ralson had lost twenty pounds since returning to the sanitarium. His face was yellow and wrinkled; the face of a man who had suddenly become sixty.

Blaustein said, "Will the test be starting soon?"

Darrity said, "It looks as if they're starting now."

He turned and leaned on the rail. Blaustein took Ralson's elbow and began leading him away, but Darrity said, softly, "Stay here, doc. I don't want you wandering about."

Blaustein looked across the laboratory. Men were standing about with the uncomfortable air of having turned half to stone. He could recognise Grant, tall and gaunt, moving his hand slowly to light a cigarette, then changing his mind and putting lighter and cigarette in his pocket. The young men at the control panels waited tensely.

Then there was a low humming and the faint smell of ozone filled the air.

Ralson said, harshly, "Look!"

Blaustein and Darrity looked along the pointing finger. The Projector seemed to flicker. It was as though there were heated air rising between it and them.

An iron ball came swinging down pendulum fashion and passed through the flickering area.

86

"It slowed up, no?" said Blaustein, excitedly.

Ralson nodded, "They're measuring the height of rise on the other side to calculate the loss of momentum. Fools! I *said* it would work." He was speaking with obvious difficulty.

Blaustein said, "Just watch, Dr. Ralson. I would not allow myself to grow needlessly excited."

The pendulum was stopped in its swinging, drawn up. The flickering about the Projector became a little more intense and the iron sphere arced down once again.

Over and over again, and each time, the sphere's motion was slowed with more of a jerk. It made a clearly audible sound as it struck the flicker. And eventually, it *bounced*. First, soggily, as though it hit putty, and then ringingly, as though it hit steel, so that the noise filled the place.

They drew back the pendulum bob and used it no longer. The Projector could hardly be seen behind the haze that surrounded it.

Grant gave an order and the odor of ozone was suddenly sharp and pungent. There was a cry from the assembled observers; each one exclaiming to his neighbor. A dozen fingers were pointing.

Blaustein leaned over the railing, as excited as the rest. Where the Projector had been, there was now only a huge semiglobular mirror. It was perfectly and beautifully clear. He could see himself in it, a small man standing on a balcony that curved up on each side. He could see the fluorescent lights reflected in spots of glowing illumination. It was wonderfully sharp.

He was shouting, "Look, Ralson. It is reflecting energy. It is reflecting light waves like a mirror. Ralson—"

He turned, "Ralson! Inspector, where is Ralson?"

"What?" Darrity whirled, "I haven't seen him."

He looked about wildly, "Well, he won't get away. No way of getting out of here now. You take the other side." And then he clapped hand to thigh, fumbled for a moment in his pocket, and said, "My knife is gone."

Blaustein found him. He was inside the small office belonging to Hal Ross. It led off the balcony, but under the circumstances, of course, it had been deserted. Ross himself was not even an observer. A senior mechanic need not observe. But his office would do very well for the final end of the long fight against suicide.

Blaustein stood in the doorway for a sick moment, then turned. He caught Darrity's eye as the latter emerged from a similar

87

office a hundred feet down the balcony. He beckoned, and Darrity came at a run—

Dr. Grant was trembling with excitement. He had taken two puffs at each of two cigarettes and trodden each underfoot thereafter. He was fumbling with the third now.

He was saying, "This is better than any of us could possibly have hoped. We'll have the gun-fire test tomorrow. I'm sure of the result now, but we've planned it; we'll go through with it. We'll skip the small arms and start with bazooka levels. Or maybe not. It might be necessary to construct a special testing structure to take care of the ricocheting problem."

He discarded his third cigarette.

A general said, "We'd have to try a literal atom-bombing, of course."

"Naturally. Arrangements have already been made to build a mock-city at Eniwetok. We could build a generator on the spot and drop the bomb. There'd be animals inside."

"And you really think the Field in full power would hold the bomb?"

"It's not just that, general. There'd be no noticeable Field when the bomb is dropped. The radiation of the plutonium would have to energize the Field before explosion. As we did here in the last step. That's the essence of it all."

"You know," said a Princeton professor, "I see disadvantages, too. When the Field is on full, anything it protects is in total darkness, as far as the sun is concerned. Besides that, it strikes me that the enemy can adopt the practice of dropping harmless radioactive missiles to set off the Field at frequent intervals. It would have nuisance value and be a considerable drain on our Pile as well."

"Nuisances," said Grant, "can be survived. These difficulties will be met eventually, I'm sure, now that the main problem has been solved."

The British observer had worked his way toward Grant and was shaking hands. He said, "I feel better about London already. I cannot help but wish your government would allow me to see the complete plans. What I have seen strikes me as completely ingenious. It seems obvious now, of course, but how did anyone ever come to think of it?"

Grant smiled, "That question has been asked before with reference to Dr. Ralson's devices—"

He turned at the touch of a hand upon his shoulder, "Dr. Blaustein! I had nearly forgotten. Here, I want to talk to you."

He dragged the small psychiatrist to one side and hissed in his ear, "Listen, can you persuade Ralson to be introduced to these people. This is his triumph."

Blaustein said, "Ralson is dead."

"*What!*"

"Can you leave these people for a time?"

"Yes . . . yes—Gentlemen, you will excuse me for a few minutes?"

He hurried off with Blaustein.

The Federal men had already taken over. Unobtrusively, they barred the doorway to Ross' office. Outside there were the milling crowd discussing the answer to Alamogordo that they had just witnessed. Inside, unknown to them, was the death of the answerer. The G-men barrier divided to allow Grant and Blaustein to enter. It closed behind them again.

For a moment. Grant raised the sheet. He said, "He looks peaceful."

"I would say—happy," said Blaustein.

Darrity said, colorlessly, "The suicide weapon was my own knife. It was my negligence; it will be reported as such."

"No, no," said Blaustein, "that would be useless. He was my patient and I am responsible. In any case, he would not have lived another week. Since he invented the Projector, he was a dying man."

Grant said, "How much of this has been placed in the Federal files? Can't we forget all about his madness?"

"I'm afraid not, Dr. Grant," said Darrity.

"I have told him the whole story," said Blaustein, sadly.

Grant looked from one to the other, "I'll speak to the Director. I'll go to the President, if necessary. I don't see that there need be any mention of suicide or of madness. He'll get full publicity as inventor of the Field Projector. It's the least we can do for him." His teeth were gritting.

Blaustein said, "He left a note."

"A note?"

Darrity handed him a sheet of paper and said, "Suicides almost always do. This is one reason the doctor told me about what really killed Ralson."

The note was addressed to Blaustein and it went:

"The Projector works; I knew it would. The bargain is done.

You've got it and you don't need me any more. So I'll go. You needn't worry about the human race, doc. You were right. They've bred us too long; they've taken too many chances. We're out of the culture now and they won't be able to stop us. I know. That's all I can say. I know."

He had signed his name quickly and then underneath there was one scrawled line, and it said:

"Provided enough men are penicillin-resistant."

Grant made a motion to crumple the paper, but Darrity held out a quick hand.

"For the record, doctor," he said.

Grant gave it to him and said, "Poor Ralson! He died believing all that trash."

Blaustein nodded, "So he did. Ralson will be given a great funeral, I suppose, and the fact of his invention will be publicized without the madness and the suicide. But the government men will remain interested in his mad theories. They may not be so mad, no, Mr. Darrity?"

"That's ridiculous, doctor," said Grant. "There isn't a scientist on the job who has shown the least uneasiness about it at all."

"Tell him, Mr. Darrity," said Blaustein.

Darrity said, "There has been another suicide. No, no none of the scientists. No one with a degree. It happened this morning, and we investigated because we thought it might have some connection with today's test, There didn't seem any, and we were going to keep it quiet till the test was over. Only now there seems to be a connection.

"The man who died was just a guy with a wife and three kids. No reason to die. No history of mental illness. He threw himself under a car. We have witnesses, and it's certain he did it on purpose. He didn't die right away and they got a doctor to him. He was horribly mangled, but his last few words were, 'I feel much better now' and he died."

"But who was he?" cried Grant.

"Hal Ross. The guy who actually built the Projector. The guy whose office this is."

Blaustein walked to the window. The evening sky was darkening into starriness.

He said, "The man knew nothing about Ralson's views. He had never spoken to Ralson, Mr. Darrity tells me. Scientists are probably resistant as a whole. They must be or they are quickly driven out of the profession. Ralson was an exception, a penicillin-sensitive who insisted on remaining. You see what happened to him.

But what about the others; those who have remained in walks of life where there is no constant weeding out of the sensitive ones. How much of humanity *is* penicillin-resistant?"

"You *believe* Ralson," asked Grant in horror.

"I don't really know."

Blaustein looked at the stars.

Incubators?

The C-Chute

Even from the cabin into which he and the other passengers had been herded, Colonel Anthony Windham could still catch the essence of the battle's progress. For a while, there was silence, no jolting, which meant the spaceships were fighting at astronomical distance in a duel of energy blasts and powerful force-field defenses.

He knew that could have only one end. Their Earth ship was only an armed merchantman and his glimpse of the Kloro enemy just before he had been cleared off deck by the crew was sufficient to show it to be a light cruiser.

And in less than half an hour, there came those hard little shocks he was waiting for. The passengers swayed back and forth as the ship pitched and veered, as though it were an ocean liner in a storm. But space was calm and silent as ever. It was their pilot sending desperate bursts of steam through the steam tubes, so that by reaction the ship would be sent rolling and tumbling. It could only mean that the inevitable had occurred. The Earth ship's screens had been drained and it no longer dared withstand a direct hit.

Colonel Windham tried to steady himself with his aluminium cane. He was thinking that he was an old man; that he had spent his life in the militia and had never seen a battle: that now, with a battle going on around him, he was old and fat and lame and had no men under his command.

They would be boarding soon, those Kloro monsters. It was their way of fighting. They would be handicapped by spacesuits and their casualties would be high, but they wanted the Earth ship. Windham considered the passengers. For a moment, he thought, *if they were armed and I could lead them—*

He abandoned the thought. Porter was in an obvious state of funk and the young boy, Leblanc, was hardly better. The Polyorketes brothers—dash it, he *couldn't* tell them apart— huddled in a corner speaking only to one another. Mullen was a different matter. He sat perfectly erect, with no signs of fear or any other emotion in his face. But the man was just about five feet tall and had undoubtedly never held a gun of any sort in his hands in all his life. He could do nothing.

And there was Stuart, with his frozen half-smile and the high-pitched sarcasm which saturated all he said. Windham looked side-long at Stuart now as Stuart sat there, pushing his dead-white hands through his sandy hair. With those artificial hands he was useless, anyway.

Windham felt the shuddering vibration of ship-to-ship contact; and in five minutes, there was the noise of the fight through the corridors. One of the Polyorketes brothers screamed and dashed for the door. The other called, "Aristides! Wait!" and hurried after.

It happened so quickly. Aristides was out the door and into the corridor, running in brainless panic. A carbonizer glowed briefly and there was never even a scream. Windham, from the doorway, turned in horror at the blackened stump of what was left. Strange —a lifetime in uniform and he had never before seen a man killed in violence.

It took the combined force of the rest to carry the other brother back struggling into the room.

The noise of battle subsided.

Stuart said, "That's it. They'll put a prize crew of two aboard and take us to one of their home planets. We're prisoners of war, naturally."

"Only two of the Kloros will stay aboard?" asked Windham, astonished.

Stuart said, "It is their custom. Why do you ask, Colonel? Thinking of leading a gallant raid to retake the ship?"

Windham flushed. "Simply a point of information, dash it." But the dignity and tone of authority he tried to assume failed him, he knew. He was simply an old man with a limp.

And Stuart was probably right. He had lived among the Kloros and knew their ways.

John Stuart had claimed from the beginning that the Kloros were gentlemen. Twenty-four hours of imprisonment had passed, and now he repeated the statement as he flexed the fingers of his hands and watched the crinkles come and go in the soft artiplasm.

He enjoyed the unpleasant reaction it aroused in the others. People were made to be punctured; windy bladders, all of them. And they had hands of the same stuff as their bodies.

There was Anthony Windham, in particular. Colonel Windham he called himself, and Stuart was willing to believe it. A retired colonel who had probably drilled a home guard militia on a village green, forty years ago, with such lack of distinction that he was not called back to service in any capacity, even during the emergency of Earth's first interstellar war.

"Dashed unpleasant thing to be saying about the enemy, Stuart. Don't know that I like your attitude." Windham seemed to push the words through his clipped mustache. His head had been shaven, too, in imitation of the current military style, but now a gray stubble was beginning to show about a centered bald patch. His flabby cheeks dragged downward. That and the fine red lines on his thick nose gave him a somewhat undone appearance, as though he had been wakened too suddenly and too early in the morning.

Stuart said, "Nonsense. Just reverse the present situation. Suppose an Earth warship had taken a Kloro liner. What do you think would have happened to any Kloro civilians aboard?"

"I'm sure the Earth fleet would observe all the interstellar rules of war," Windham said stiffly.

"Except that there aren't any. If we landed a prize crew on one of their ships, do you think we'd take the trouble to maintain a chlorine atmosphere for the benefit of the survivors; allow them to keep their non-contraband possessions; give them the use of the most comfortable stateroom, etcetera, etcetera, etcetera?"

Ben Porter said, "Oh, shut up, for God's sake. If I hear your etcetera, etcetera once again, I'll go nuts."

Stuart said, "Sorry!" He wasn't.

Porter was scarcely responsible. His thin face and beaky nose glistened with perspiration, and he kept biting the inside of his cheek until he suddenly winced. He put his tongue against the sore spot, which made him look even more clownish.

Stuart was growing weary of baiting them. Windham was too flabby a target and Porter could do nothing but writhe. The rest were silent. Demetrios Polyorketes was off in a world of silent internal grief for the moment. He had not slept the night before, most probably. At least, whenever Stuart woke to change his position—he himself had been rather restless—there had been Polyorketes' thick mumble from the next cot. It said many things, but the moan to which it returned over and over again was, "Oh, my brother!"

He sat dumbly on his cot now, his red eyes rolling at the other prisoners out of his broad swarthy, unshaven face. As Stuart watched, his face sank into calloused palms so that only his mop

94

of crisp and curly black hair could be seen. He rocked gently, but now that they were all awake, he made no sound.

Claude Leblanc was trying, very unsuccessfully, to read a letter. He was the youngest of the six, scarcely out of college, returning to Earth to get married. Stuart had found him that morning weeping quietly, his pink and white face flushed and blotched as though it were a heartbroken child's. He was very fair, with almost a girl's beauty about his large blue eyes and full lips. Stuart wondered what kind of girl it was who had promised to be his wife. He had seen her picture. Who on the ship had not? She had the characterless prettiness that makes all pictures of fiancees indistinguishable. It seemed to Stuart that if he were a girl, however, he would want someone a little more pronouncedly masculine.

That left only Randolph Mullen. Stuart frankly did not have the least idea what to make of him. He was the only one of the six that had been on the Arcturian worlds for any length of time. Stuart, himself, for instance, had been there only long enough to give a series of lectures on astronautical engineering at the provincial engineering institute. Colonel Windham had been on a Cook's tour; Porter was trying to buy concentrated alien vegetables for his canneries on Earth; and the Polyorketes brothers had attempted to establish themselves in Arcturus as truck farmers and, after two growing seasons, gave it up, had somehow unloaded at a profit, and were returning to Earth.

Randolph Mullen, however, had been in the Arcturian system for seventeen years. How did voyagers discover so much about one another so quickly? As far as Stuart knew, the little man had scarcely spoken aboard ship. He was unfailingly polite, always stepped to one side to allow another to pass, but his entire vocabularly appeared to consist only of "Thank you" and Pardon me." Yet the word had gone around that this was his first trip to Earth in seventeen years.

He was a little man, very precise, almost irritatingly so. Upon awaking that morning, he had made his cot neatly, shaved, bathed and dressed. The habit of years seemed not in the least disturbed by the fact that he was a prisoner of the Kloros now. He was unobtrusive about it, it had to be admitted, and gave no impression of disapproving of the sloppiness of the others. He simply sat there, almost apologetic, trussed in his overconservative clothing, and hands loosely clasped in his lap. The thin line of hair on his upper lip, far from adding character to his face, absurdly increased its primness.

He looked like someone's idea of a caricature of a bookkeeper.

And the queer thing about it all, Stuart thought, was that that was exactly what he was. He had noticed it on the registry—Randolph Fluellen Mullen; occupation, bookkeeper; employers, Prime Paper Box Co.; 27 Tobias Avenue, New Warsaw, Arcturus II.

"Mr. Stuart?"

Stuart looked up. It was Leblanc, his lower lip trembling slightly. Stuart tried to remember how one went about being gentle. He said, "What is it, Leblanc?"

"Tell me, when will they let us go?"

"How should I know?"

"Everyone says you lived on a Kloro planet, and just now you said they were gentlemen."

"Well, yes. But even gentlemen fight wars in order to win. Probably, we'll be interned for the duration."

"But that could be *years!* Margaret is waiting. She'll think I'm *dead!*"

"I suppose they'll allow messages to be sent through once we're on their planet."

Porter's hoarse voice sounded in agitation. "Look here, if you know so much about these devils, what will they do to us while we're interned? What will they feed us? Where will they get oxygen for us? They'll kill us, I tell you." And as an afterthought, "I've got a wife waiting for me, too," he added.

But Stuart had heard him speaking of his wife in the days before the attack. He wasn't impressed. Porter's nail-bitten fingers were pulling and plucking at Stuart's sleeve. Stuart drew away in sharp revulsion. He couldn't stand those ugly hands, It angered him to desperation that such monstrosities should be real while his own white and perfectly shaped hands were only mocking imitations grown out of an alien latex.

He said, "They won't kill us. If they were going to, they would have done it before now. Look, we capture Kloros too, you know, and it's just a matter of common sense to treat your prisoners decently if you want the other side to be decent to your men. They'll do their best. The food may not be very good, but they're better chemists than we are. It's what they're best at. They'll know exactly what food factors we'll need and how many calories. We'll live. They'll see to that."

Windham rumbled, "You sound more and more like a blasted greenie sympathizer, Stuart. It turns my stomach to hear an

Earthman speak well of the green fellas the way you've been doing. Burn it, man, where's your loyalty?"

"My loyalty's where it belongs. With honesty and decency, regardless of the shape of the being it appears in." Stuart held up his hands. "See these? Kloros made them. I lived on one of their planets for six months. My hands were mangled in the conditioning machinery of my own quarters. I thought the oxygen supply they gave me was a little poor—it wasn't, by the way—and I tried making the adjustments on my own. It was my fault. You should never trust yourself with the machines of another culture. By the time someone among the Kloros could put on an atmosphere suit and get to me, it was too late to save my hands.

"They grew these artiplasm things for me and operated. You know what that meant? It meant designing equipment and nutrient solutions that would work in oxygen atmosphere. It meant that their surgeons had to perform a delicate operation while dressed in atmosphere suits. And now I've got hands again." He laughed harshly, and clenched them into weak fists. "Hands—"

Windham said, "And you'd sell your loyalty to Earth for that?"

"Sell my loyalty? You're mad. For years, I hated the Kloros for this. I was a master pilot on the Trans-Galactic Spacelines before it happened. Now? Desk job. Or an occasional lecture. It took me a long time to pin the fault on myself and to realize that the only role played by the Kloros was a decent one. They have their code of ethics, and it's as good as ours. If it weren't for the stupidity of some of their people—and, by God, of some of ours—we wouldn't be at war. And after it's over—"

Polyorketes was on his feet. His thick fingers curved inward before him and his dark eyes glittered. "I don't like what you say, mister."

"Why don't you?"

"Because you talk too nice about these damned green bastards. The Kloros were good to you, eh? Well, they weren't good to my brother. They killed him. I think maybe I kill you, you damned greenie spy."

And he charged.

Stuart barely had time to raise his arms to meet the infuriated farmer. He gasped out, "What the hell—" as he caught one wrist and heaved a shoulder to block the other which groped toward his throat.

His artiplasm hand gave way. Polyorketes wrenched free with scarcely an effort.

Windham was bellowing incoherently, and Leblanc was calling

out in his seedy voice, "Stop it! Stop it!" But it was little Mullen who threw his arms about the farmer's neck from behind and pulled with all his might. He was not very effective; Polyorketes seemed scarcely aware of the little man's weight upon his back. Mullen's feet left the floor so that he tossed helplessly to right and left. But he held his grip and it hampered Polyorketes sufficiently to allow Stuart to break free long enough to grasp Windham's aluminium cane.

He said, "Stay away, Polyorketes."

He was gasping for breath and fearful of another rush. The hollow aluminium cylinder was scarcely heavy enough to accomplish much, but it was better than having only his weak hands to defend himself with.

Mullen has loosed his hold and was now circling cautiously, his breathing roughened and his jacket in disarray.

Polyorketes, for a moment, did not move. He stood there, his shaggy head bent low. Then he said, "It is no use. I must kill Kloros. Just watch your tongue, Stuart. If it keeps on rattling too much, you're liable to get hurt. Really hurt, I mean."

Stuart passed a forearm over his forehead and thrust the cane back to Windham, who seized it with his left hand, while mopping his bald pate vigorously with a handkerchief in his right.

Windham said, "Gentlemen, we must avoid this. It lowers our prestige. We must remember the common enemy. We are Earthmen and we must act what we are—the ruling race of the Galaxy. We dare not demean ourselves before the lesser breeds."

"Yes, Colonel," said Stuart, wearily. "Give us the rest of the speech tomorrow."

He turned to Mullen, "I want to say thanks."

He was uncomfortable about it, but he had to. The little accountant had surprised him completely.

But Mullen said in a dry voice that scarcely raised above a whisper, "Don't thank me, Mr. Stuart. It was the logical thing to do. If we are to be interned, we would need you as an interpreter, perhaps, one who would understand the Kloros."

Stuart stiffened. It was, he thought, too much the bookkeeper type of reasoning, too logical, too dry of juice. Present risk and ultimate advantage. The assets and debits balanced neatly. He would have liked Mullen to leap to his defense out of—well, out of what? Out of pure, unselfish decency?

Stuart laughed silently at himself. He was beginning to expect idealism of human beings, rather than good, straightforward, self-centered motivation.

Polyorketes was numb. His sorrow and rage were like acid inside him, but they had no words to get out. If he were Stuart, big-mouth, white-hands Stuart, he could talk and talk and maybe feel better. Instead, he had to sit there with half of him dead; with no brother, no Aristides—

It had happened so quickly. If he could only go back and have one second more warning, so that he might snatch Aristides, hold him, save him.

But mostly he hated the Kloros. Two months ago, he had hardly ever heard of them, and now he hated them so hard, he would be glad to die if he could kill a few.

He said, without looking up, "What happened to start this war, eh?"

He was afraid Stuart's voice would answer. He hated Stuart's voice. But it was Windham, the bald one.

Windham said, "The immediate cause, sir, was a dispute over mining concessions in the Wyandotte system. The Kloros had poached on Earth property."

"Room for both, Colonel!"

Polyorketes looked up at that, snarling. Stuart could not be kept quiet for long. He was speaking again; the cripple-hand, wiseguy, Kloros-lover.

Stuart was saying, "Is that anything to fight over, Colonel? We can't use one another's worlds. Their chlorine planets are useless to us and our oxygen ones are useless to them. Chlorine is deadly to us and oxygen is deadly to them. There's no way we could maintain permanent hostility. Our races just don't coincide. Is there reason to fight then because both races want to dig iron out of the same airless planetoids when there are millions like them in the Galaxy?"

Windham said, "There is the question of planetary honor—"

"Planetary fertilizer. How can it excuse a ridiculous war like this one? It can only be fought on outposts. It has come down to a series of holding actions and eventually settled by negotiations that might just as easily have been worked out in the first place. Neither we nor the Kloros will gain a thing."

Grudgingly, Polyorketes found that he agreed with Stuart. What did he and Aristides care where Earth or the Kloros got their iron?

Was that something for Aristides to die over?

The little warning buzzer sounded.

Polyorketes' head shot up and he rose slowly, his lips drawing back. Only one thing could be at the door. He waited, arms tense,

99

fists balled. Stuart was edging toward him. Polyorketes saw that and laughed to himself. Let the Kloro come in, and Stuart, along with all the rest, could not stop him.

Wait, Aristides, wait just a moment, and a fraction of revenge will be paid back.

The door opened and a figure entered, completely swathed in a shapeless, billowing travesty of a spacesuit.

An odd, unnatural, but not entirely unpleasant voice began, "It is with some misgivings Earthmen, that my companion and myself—"

It ended abruptly as Polyorketes, with a roar, charged once again. There was no science in the lunge. It was sheer bull-momentum. Dark head low, burly arms spread out with the hairtufted fingers in choking position, he clumped on. Stuart was whirled to one side before he had a chance to intervene, and was spun tumbling across a cot.

The Kloro might have, without undue exertion, straight-armed Polyorketes to a halt, or stepped aside, allowing the whirlwind to pass. He did neither. With a rapid movement, a hand-weapon was up and a gentle pinkish line of radiance connected it with the plunging Earthman. Polyorketes stumbled and crashed down, his body maintaining its last curved position, one foot raised, as though a lightning paralysis had taken place. It toppled to one side and he lay there, eyes all alive and wild with rage.

The Kloro said, "He is not permanently hurt." He seemed not to resent the offered violence. Then he began again, "It is with some misgiving, Earthmen, that my companion and myself were made aware of a certain commotion in this room. Are you in any need which we can satisfy?"

Stuart was angrily nursing his knee which he had scraped in colliding with the cot. He said, "No thank you, Kloro."

"Now, look here," puffed Windham, "this is a dashed outrage. We demand that our release be arranged."

The Kloro's tiny, insectlike head turned in the fat old man's direction. He was not a pleasant sight to anyone unused to him. He was about the height of an Earthman, but the top of him consisted of a thin stalk of a neck with a head that was the merest swelling. It consisted of a blunt triangular proboscis in front and two bulging eyes on either side. That was all. There was no brain pan and no brain. What corresponded to the brain in a Kloro was located in what would be an Earthly abdomen, leaving the head as a mere sensory organ. The Kloro's spacesuit followed the outlines

100

of the head more or less faithfully, the two eyes being exposed by two clear semicircles of glass, which looked faintly green because of the chlorine atmosphere inside.

One of the eyes was now cocked squarely at Windham, who quivered uncomfortably under the glance, but insisted, "You have no right to hold us prisoner. We are noncombatants."

The Kloro's voice, sounding thoroughly artificial, came from a small attachment of chromium mesh on what served as its chest. The voice box was manipulated by compressed air under the control of one or two of the many delicate, forked tendrils that radiated from two circles about its upper body and were, mercifully enough, hidden by the suit.

The voice said, "Are you serious, Earthman? Surely you have heard of war and rules of war and prisoners of war."

It looked about, shifting eyes with quick jerks of its head, staring at a particular object first with one, then with another. It was Stuart's understanding that each eye transferred a separate message to the abdominal brain, which had to coordinate the two to obtain full information.

Windham had nothing to say. No one had. The Kloro, its four main limbs, roughly arms and legs in pairs, had a vaguely human appearance under the masking of the suit, if you looked no higher than its chest, but there was no way of telling what it felt.

They watched it turn and leave.

Porter coughed and said in a strangled voice, "God, smell that chlorine. If they don't do something, we'll all die of rotted lungs."

Stuart said, "Shut up. There isn't enough chlorine in the air to make a mosquito sneeze, and what there is will be swept out in two minutes. Besides, a little chlorine is good for you. It may kill your cold virus."

Windham coughed and said, "Stuart, I feel that you might have said something to your Kloro friend about releasing us. You are scarcely as bold in their presence, dash it, as you are once they are gone."

"You heard what the creature said, Colonel. We're prisoners of war, and prisoner exchanges are negotiated by diplomats. We'll just have to wait."

Leblanc, who had turned pasty white at the entrance of the Kloro, rose and hurried into the privy. There was a sound of retching.

An uncomfortable silence fell while Stuart tried to think of something to say to cover the unpleasant sound. Mullen filled in.

He rummaged through a little box he had taken from under his pillow.

He said, "Perhaps Mr. Leblanc had better take a sedative before retiring. I have a few. I'd be glad to give him one." He explained his generosity immediately, "Otherwise he may keep the rest of us awake, you see."

"Very logical," said Stuart, dryly. "You'd better save one for Sir Launçelot here; save half a dozen." He walked to where Polyorketes still sprawled and knelt at his side. "Comfortable, baby?"

Windham said, "Deuced poor taste speaking like that, Stuart."

"Well, if you're so concerned about him, why don't you and Porter hoist him onto his cot?"

He helped them do so. Polyorketes' arms were trembling erratically now. From what Stuart knew of the Kloro's nerve weapon, the man should be in an agony of pins and needles about now.

Stuart said, "And don't be too gentle with him, either. The damned fool might have gotten us all killed. And for what?"

He pushed Polyorketes' stiff carcass to one side and sat at the edge of the cot. He said, "Can you hear me, Polyorketes?"

Polyorketes' eyes gleamed. An arm lifted abortively and fell back.

"Okay then, listen. Don't try anything like that again. The next time it may be the finish for all of us. If you had been a Kloro and he had been an Earthman, we'd be dead now. So just get one thing through your skull. We're sorry about your brother and it's a rotten shame, but it was his own fault."

Polyorketes tried to heave and Stuart pushed him back.

"No, you keep on listening," he said. "Maybe this is the only time I'll get to talk to you when you have to listen. Your brother had no right leaving passenger's quarters. There was no place for him to go. He just got in the way of our own men. We don't even know for certain that it was a Kloro gun that killed him. It might have been one of our own."

"Oh, I say, Stuart," objected Windham.

Stuart whirled at him. "Do you have proof it wasn't? Did you see the shot? Could you tell from what was left of the body whether it was Kloro energy or Earth energy?"

Polyorketes found his voice, driving his unwilling tongue into a fuzzy verbal snarl. "Damned stinking greenie bastard."

"Me?" said Stuart. "I know what's going on in your mind, Polyorketes. You think that when the paralysis wears off, you'll ease your feelings by slamming me around. Well, if you do, it will probably be curtains for all of us."

He rose, put his back against the wall. For the moment, he was fighting all of them. "None of you know the Kloros the way I do. The physical differences you see are not important. The differences in the temperament are. They don't understand our views on sex, for instance. To them, it's just a biological reflex like breathing. They attach no importance to it. But they *do* attach importance to social groupings. Remember, their evolutionary ancestors had lots in common with our insects. They always assume that any group of Earthmen they find together makes up a social unit.

"That means just about everything to them. I don't understand exactly *what* it means. No Earthman can. But the result is that they never break up a group, just as we don't separate a mother and her children if we can help it. One of the reasons they're treating us with kid gloves right now is that they imagine we're all broken up over the fact that they killed one of us, and they feel guilt about it.

"But this is what you'll have to remember. We're going to be interned together and *kept* together for duration. I don't like the thought. I wouldn't have picked any of you for co-internees and I'm pretty sure none of you would have picked me. But there it is. The Kloros could never understand that our being together on the ship is only accidental.

"That means we've got to get along somehow. That's not just goodie-goodie talk about birds in their little nests agreeing. What do you think would have happened if the Kloros had come in earlier and found Polyorketes and myself trying to kill each other? You don't know? Well, what do you suppose *you* would think of a mother you caught trying to kill her children?

"That's it then. They would have killed every one of us as a bunch of Kloro-type perverts and monsters. Got that? How about you, Polyorketes? Have *you* got it? So let's call names if we have to, but let's keep our hands to ourselves. And now, if none of you mind, I'll massage my hands back into shape—these synthetic hands that I got from the Kloros and that one of my own kind tried to mangle again."

For Claude Leblanc, the worst was over. He had been sick enough; sick with many things; but sick most of all over having ever left the Earth. It had been a great thing to go to college off Earth. It had been an adventure and had taken him away from

103

his mother. Somehow, he had been sneakingly glad to make that escape after the first month of frightened adjustment.

And then on the summer holidays, he had been no longer Claude, the shy-spoken scholar, but Leblanc, space traveler. He had swaggered the fact for all it was worth. It made him feel such a man to talk of stars and Jumps and the customs and environment of other worlds; it had given him courage with Margaret. She had loved him for the dangers he had undergone—

Except that this had been the first one, really, and he had not done so well. He knew it and was ashamed and wished he were like Stuart.

He used the excuse of mealtime to approach. He said, "Mr. Stuart."

Stuart looked up and said shortly, "How do you feel?"

Leblanc felt himself blush. He blushed easily and the effort not to blush only made it worse. He said, "Much better, thank you. We are eating. I thought I'd bring you your ration."

Stuart took the offered can. It was standard space ration; thoroughly synthetic, concentrated, nourishing and, somehow, unsatisfying. It heated automatically when the can was opened, but could be eaten cold, if necessary. Though a combined fork-spoon utensil was enclosed, the ration was of a consistency that made the use of fingers practical and not particularly messy.

Stuart said, "Did you hear my little speech?"

"Yes, sir. I want you to know you can count on me."

"Well, good. Now go and eat."

"May I eat here?"

"Suit yourself."

For a moment, they ate in silence, and then Leblanc burst out, "You are so sure of yourself, Mr. Stuart! It must be very wonderful to be like that!"

"Sure of myself? Thanks, but there's your self-assured one."

Leblanc followed the direction of the nod in surprise. "Mr. Mullen? That little man? Oh, no!"

"You don't think he's self-assured?"

Leblanc shook his head. He looked at Stuart intently to see if he could detect humor in his expression. "That one is just cold. He had no emotion in him. He's like a little machine. I find him repulsive. You're different, Mr. Stuart. You have it all inside, but you control it. I would like to be like that."

And as though attracted by the magnetism of the mention, even though unheard, of his name, Mullen joined them. His can of

104

ration was barely touched. It was still steaming gently as he squatted opposite them.

His voice had its usual quality of furtively rustling underbrush. "How long, Mr. Stuart, do you think the trip will take?"

"Can't say, Mullen. They'll undoubtedly be avoiding the usual trade routes and they'll be making more Jumps through hyperspace than usual to throw off possible pursuit. I wouldn't be surprised if it took as long as a week. Why do you ask? I presume you have a very practical and logical reason?"

"Why, yes. Certainly." He seemed quite shellbacked to sarcasm. He said, "It occurred to me that it might be wise to ration the rations, so to speak."

"We've got enough food and water for a month. I checked on that first thing."

"I see. In that case, I will finish the can." He did, using the all-purpose utensil daintily and patting a handkerchief against his unstained lips from time to time.

Polyorketes struggled to his feet some two hours later. He swayed a bit, looking like the Spirit of Hangover. He did not try to come closer to Stuart, but spoke from where he stood.

He said, "You stinking greenie spy, you watch yourself."

"You heard what I said before, Polyorketes."

"I heard. But I also heard what you said about Aristides. I won't bother with you, because you're a bag of nothing but noisy air. But wait, someday you'll blow air in one face too many and it will be let out of you."

"I'll wait," said Stuart.

Windham hobbled over, leaning heavily on his cane. "Now, now," he called with a wheezing joviality that overlaid his sweating anxiety so thinly as to emphasize it. "We're all Earthmen, dash it. Got to remember that; keep it as a glowing light of inspiration. Never let down before the blasted Kloros. We've got to forget private feuds and remember only that we are Earthmen united against alien blighters."

Stuart's comment was unprintable.

Porter was right behind Windham. He had been in a close conference with the shaven-headed colonel for an hour, and now he said with indignation. "It doesn't help to be a wiseguy, Stuart. You listen to the colonel. We've been doing some hard thinking about the situation."

He had washed some of the grease off his face, wet his hair and slicked it back. It did not remove the little tic on his right cheek

105

just at the point where his lips ended, or make his hangnail hands more attractive in appearance.

"All right, Colonel," said Stuart. "What's on your mind?"

Windham said, "I'd prefer to have all the men together."

"Okay, call them."

Leblanc hurried over; Mullen approached with greater deliberation.

Stuart said, "You want that fellow?" He jerked his head at Polyorketes.

"Why, yes. Mr. Polyorketes, may we have you, old fella?"

"Ah, leave me alone."

"Go ahead," said Stuart, "leave him alone. I don't want him."

"No, no," said Windham. "This is a matter for all Earthmen. Mr. Polyorketes, we must have you."

Polyorketes rolled off one side of his cot. "I'm close enough. I can hear you."

Windham said to Stuart, "Would they—the Kloros, I mean—have this room wired?"

"No," said Stuart. "Why should they?"

"Are you sure?"

"Of course I'm sure. They didn't know what happened when Polyorketes jumped me. They just heard the thumping when it started rattling the ship."

"Maybe they were trying to give us the impression the room wasn't wired."

"Listen, Colonel, I've never known a Kloro to tell a deliberate lie—"

Polyorketes interrupted calmly, "That lump of noise just *loves* the Kloros."

Windham said hastily, "Let's not begin that. Look, Stuart, Porter and I have been discussing matters and we have decided that you know the Kloros well enough to think of some way of getting us back to Earth."

"It happens that you're wrong. I can't think of any way."

"Maybe there is some way we can take the ship back from the blasted green fellas," suggested Windham. "Some weakness they may have. Dash it, you know what I mean."

"Tell me, Colonel, what are you after? Your own skin or Earth's welfare?"

"I resent that question. I'll have you know that while I'm as careful of my own life as anyone has a right to be, I'm thinking of Earth primarily. And I think that's true of all of us."

"Damn right," said Porter, instantly. Leblanc looked anxious,

106

Polyorketes resentful; and Mullen had no expression at all.

"Good," said Stuart. "Of course, I don't think we can take the ship. They're armed and we aren't. But there's this. You know why the Kloros took this ship intact. It's because they need ships. They may be better chemists than Earthmen are, but Earthmen are better astronautical engineers. We have bigger, better and more ships. In fact, if our crew had had a proper respect for military axioms in the first place, they would have blown the ship up as soon as it looked as though the Kloros were going to board."

Leblanc looked horrified. "And kill the passengers?"

"Why not? You heard what the good colonel said. Every one of us puts his own lousy little life after Earth's interests. What good are we to Earth alive right now? None at all. What harm will this ship do in Kloro hands? A hell of a lot, probably."

"Just why," asked Mullen, "did our men refuse to blow up the ship? They must have had a reason."

"They did. It's the firmest tradition of Earth's military men, that there must never be an unfavorable ratio of casualties. If we had blown ourselves up, twenty fighting men and seven civilians of Earth would be dead as compared with an enemy casualty total of zero. So what happens? We let them board, kill twenty-eight—I'm sure we killed at least that many—and let them have the ship."

"Talk, talk, talk," jeered Polyorketes.

"There's a moral to this," said Stuart. "We can't take the ship away from the Kloros. We *might* be able to rush them, though, and keep them busy long enough to allow one of us enough time to short the engines."

"What?" yelled Porter, and Windham shushed him in fright.

"Short the engines," Stuart repeated. "That would destroy the ship, of course, which is what we want to do, isn't it?"

Leblanc's lips were white. "I don't think that would work."

"We can't be sure till we try. But what have we to lose by trying?"

"Our lives, damn it!" cried Porter. "You insane maniac, you're crazy!"

"If I'm a maniac," said Stuart, "and insane to boot, then naturally I'm crazy. But just remember that if we lose our lives, which is overwhelmingly probable, we lose nothing of value to Earth; whereas if we destroy the ship, as we just barely might, we do Earth a lot of good. What patriot would hesitate? Who here would put himself ahead of his world?" He looked about in the silence. "Surely not you, Colonel Windham."

Windham coughed tremendously. "My dear man, that is not

107

the question. There must be a way to save the ship for Earth *without* losing our lives, eh?"

"All right. *You* name it."

"Let's all think about it. Now there are only two of the Kloros aboard ship. If one of us could sneak up on them and—"

"How? The rest of the ship's all filled with chlorine. We'd have to wear a spacesuit. Gravity in their part of the ship is hopped up to Kloro level, so whoever is patsy in the deal would be clumping around, metal on metal, slow and heavy. Oh, he could sneak up on them, sure—like a skunk trying to sneak downwind."

"Then we'll drop it all," Porter's voice shook. "Listen, Windham, there's not going to be any destroying the ship. My life means plenty to me and if any of you try anything like that, I'll call the Kloros. I mean it."

"Well," said Stuart, "there's hero number one."

Leblanc said, "I want to go back to Earth, but I—"

Mullen interrupted, "I don't think our chances of destroying the ship are good enough unless—"

"Heroes number two and three. What about you, Polyorketes? You would have a chance of killing two Kloros."

I want to kill them with my bare hands," growled the farmer, his heavy fists writhing. "On their planet, I will kill dozens."

"That's a nice safe promise for now. What about you, Colonel? Don't you want to march to death and glory with me?"

"Your attitude is very cynical and unbecoming, Stuart. It's obvious that if the rest are unwilling, then your plan will fall through."

"Unless I do it myself, huh?"

"You won't, do you hear?" said Porter, instantly.

"Damn right I won't," agreed Stuart. "I don't claim to be a hero. I'm just an average patriot, perfectly willing to head for any planet they take me to and sit out the war."

Mullen said, thoughtfully, "Of course, there *is* a way we could surprise the Kloros."

The statement would have dropped flat except for Polyorketes. He pointed a black-nailed, stubby forefinger and laughed harshly.

"Mr. Bookkeeper!" he said. "Mr. Bookkeeper is a big shot talker like this damned greenie spy, Stuart. All right, Mr. Bookkeeper, go ahead. You make big speeches also. Let the words roll like an empty barrel."

He turned to Stuart and repeated venomously, "Empty barrel! Cripple-hand empty barrel. No good for anything but talk."

Mullen's soft voice could make no headway until Polyorketes was through, but then he said, speaking directly to Stuart, "We might be able to reach them from outside. This room has a C-chute, I'm sure."

"What's a C-chute?" asked Leblanc.

"Well—" began Mullen, and then stopped, at a loss.

Stuart said, mockingly, "It's a euphemism, my boy. Its full name is 'casualty chute.' It doesn't get talked about, but the main rooms on any ship would have them. They're just little airlocks down which you slide a corpse. Burial at space. Always lots of sentiment and bowed heads, with the captain making a rolling speech of the type Polyorketes here wouldn't like."

Leblanc's face twisted. "Use *that* to leave the ship?"

"Why not? Superstitious?—Go on, Mullen."

The little man had waited patiently. He said, "Once outside, one could re-enter the ship by the steam-tubes. It can be done—with luck. And then you would be an unexpected visitor in the control room."

Stuart stared at him curiously. "How do you figure this out? What do *you* know about steam-tubes?"

Mullen coughed. "You mean because I'm in the paper-box business? Well—" He grew pink, waited for a moment, then made a new start in a colorless, unemotional voice. "My company, which manufactures fancy paper boxes and novelty containers, made a line of spaceship candy boxes for the juvenile trade some years ago. It was designed so that if a string were pulled, small pressure containers were punctured and jets of compressed air shot out through the mock steam-tubes, sailing the box across the room and scattering candy as it went. The sales theory was that the youngsters would find it exciting to play with the ship and fun to scramble for the candy.

"Actually, it was a complete failure. The ship would break dishes and sometimes hit another child in the eye. Worse still, the children would not only scramble for the candy but would fight over it. It was almost our worst failure. We lost thousands.

"Still, while the boxes were being designed, the entire office was extremely interested. It was like a game, very bad for efficiency and office morale. For a while, we all became steam-tube experts. I read quite a few books on ship construction. On my own time, however, not the company's"

Stuart was intrigued. He said. "You know it's a video sort of idea, but it might work if we had a hero to spare. Have we?"

"What about you?" demanded Porter, indignantly. "You go

around sneering at us with your cheap wisecracks. I don't notice you volunteering for anything."

"That's because I'm no hero, Porter. I admit it. My object is to stay alive, and shinnying down steam-tubes is no way to go about staying alive. But the rest of you are noble patriots. The Colonel says so. What about you, Colonel? You're the senior hero here."

Windham said, "If I were younger, blast it, and if you had your hands, I would take pleasure, sir, in trouncing you soundly."

"I've no doubt of it, but that's no answer."

"You know very well that at my time of life and with my leg—" he brought the flat of his hand down upon his stiff knee— "I am in no position to do anything of the sort, however, much I should wish to."

"Ah, yes," said Stuart, "and I, myself, am crippled in the hands, as Polyorketes tells me. That saves us. And what unfortunate deformities do the rest of us have?"

"Listen," cried Porter, "I want to know what this is all about. How can anyone go down the steam-tubes? What if the Kloros use them while one of us is inside?"

"Why, Porter, that's part of the sporting chance. It's where the excitement comes in."

"But he'd be boiled in the shell like a lobster."

"A pretty image, but inaccurate. The steam wouldn't be on for more than a very short time, maybe a second or two, and the suit insulation would hold that long. Besides, the jet comes scooting out at several hundred miles a minute, so that you would be blown clear of the ship before the steam could even warm you. In fact, you'd be blown quite a few miles out into space, and after that you would be quite safe from the Kloros. Of course, you couldn't get back to the ship."

Porter was sweating freely. "You don't scare me for one minute, Stuart."

"I don't? Then you're offering to go? Are you sure you've thought out what being stranded in space means? You're all alone, you know; really all alone. The steam jet will probably leave you turning or tumbling pretty rapidly. You won't feel that. You'll seem to be motionless. But all the stars will be going around and around so that they're just streaks in the sky. They won't ever stop. They won't even slow up. Then your heater will go or your oxygen will give out, and you will die very slowly. You'll have lots of time to think. Or, if you are in a hurry, you could open your suit. That wouldn't be pleasant, either. I've seen the faces of men

110

who had a torn suit happen to them accidentally, and it's pretty awful. But it would be quicker. Then—"

Porter turned and walked unsteadily away.

Stuart said, lightly, "Another failure. One act of heroism still ready to be knocked down to the highest bidder with nothing offered yet."

Polyorketes spoke up and his harsh voice roughed the words. "You keep on talking, Mr. Big Mouth. You just keep banging that empty barrel. Pretty soon, we'll kick your teeth in. There's one boy I think would be willing to do it now, eh, Mr. Porter?"

Porter's look at Stuart confirmed the truth of Polyorketes' remarks, but he said nothing.

Stuart said, "Then what about you, Polyorketes? You're the bare-hand man with guts. Want me to help you into a suit?"

"I'll ask you when I want help."

"What about you, Leblanc?"

The young man shrank away.

"Not even to get back to Margaret?"

But Leblanc could only shake his head.

"Mullen?"

"Well—I'll try."

"You'll what?"

"I said, yes, I'll try. After all, it's my idea."

Stuart looked stunned. "You're serious? How come?"

Mullen's prim mouth pursed. "Because no one else will."

"But that's no reason. Especially for you."

Mullen shrugged.

There was a thump of a cane behind Stuart. Windham brushed past.

He said, "Do you really intend to go, Mullen?"

"Yes, Colonel."

"In that case, dash it, let me shake your hand. I like you. You're an—an Earthman, by heaven. Do this, and win or die, I'll bear witness for you."

Mullen withdrew his hand awkwardly from the deep and vibrating grasp of the other.

And Stuart just stood there. He was in a very unusual position. He was, in fact, in the peculiar position of all positions in which he had most rarely found himself.

He had nothing to say.

The quality of tension had changed. The gloom and frustration had lifted a bit, and the excitement of conspiracy had replaced it.

Even Polyorketes was fingering the spacesuits and commenting briefly and hoarsely on which he considered preferable.

Mullen was having a certain amount of trouble. The suit hung rather limply upon him even though the adjustable joints had been tightened nearly to minimum. He stood there now with only the helmet to be screwed on. He wiggled his neck.

Stuart was holding the helmet with an effort. It was heavy, and his artiplasmic hands did not grip it well. He said, "Better scratch your nose if it itches. It's your last chance for a while." He didn't add, "Maybe forever," but he thought it.

Mullen said, tonelessly, "I think perhaps I had better have a spare oxygen cylinder."

"Good enough."

"With a reducing valve."

Stuart nodded. "I see what you're thinking of. If you do get blown clear of the ship, you could try to blow yourself back by using the cylinder as an action-reaction motor."

They clamped on the headpiece and buckled the spare cylinder to Mullen's waist. Polyorketes and Leblanc lifted him up to the yawning opening of the C-tube. It was ominously dark inside, the metal lining of the interior having been painted a mournful black. Stuart thought he could detect a musty odor about it, but that, he knew, was only imagination.

He stopped the proceedings when Mullen was half within the tube. He tapped upon the little man's faceplate.

"Can you hear me?"

Within, there was a nod.

"Air coming through all right? No last-minute troubles?"

Mullen lifted his armored arm in a gesture of reassurance.

"Then remember, don't use the suit-radio out there. The Kloros might pick up the signals."

Reluctantly, he stepped away. Polyorketes' brawny hands lowered Mullen until they could hear the thumping sound made by the steel-shod feet against the outer valve. The inner valve then swung shut with a dreadful finality, its beveled silicone gasket making a slight soughing noise as it crushed hard. They clamped it into place.

Stuart stood at the toggle-switch that controlled the outer valve. He threw it and the gauge that marked the air pressure within the tube fell to zero. A little pinpoint of red light warned that the outer valve was open. Then the light disappeared, the valve closed and the gauge climbed slowly to fifteen pounds again.

They opened the inner valve again and found the tube empty.

112

Polyorketes spoke first. He said, "The little son-of-a-gun. He went!" He looked wonderingly at the other. "A little fellow with guts like that."

Stuart said, "Look, we'd better get ready in here. There's just a chance that the Kloros may have detected the valves opening and closing. If so, they'll be here to investigate and we'll have to cover up."

"How?" asked Windham.

"They won't see Mullen anywhere around. We'll say he's in the head. The Kloros know that it's one of the peculiar characteristics of Earthmen that they resent intrusion on their privacy in lavatories, and they'll make no effort to check. If we can hold them off—"

"What if they wait, or if they check the spacesuits?" asked Porter.

Stuart shrugged. "Let's hope they don't. And listen, Polyorketes, don't make any fuss when they come in."

Polyorketes grunted, "With that little guy out there? What do you think I am?" He stared at Stuart without animosity, then scratched his curly hair vigorously, "You know, I laughed at him. I thought he was an old woman. It makes me ashamed."

Stuart cleared his throat. He said, "Look, I've been saying some things that maybe weren't too funny after all, now that I come to think of it. I'd like to say I'm sorry if I have."

He turned away morosely and walked toward his cot. He heard the steps behind him, felt the touch on his sleeve. He turned; it was Leblanc.

The youngster said softly, "I keep thinking that Mr. Mullen is an old man."

"Well, he's not a kid. He's about forty-five or fifty, I think."

Leblanc said, "Do you think, Mr. Stuart, that *I* should have gone, instead? I'm the youngest here. I don't like the thought of having let an old man go in my place. It makes me feel like the devil."

"I know. If he dies, it will be too bad."

"But he volunteered. We didn't make him, did we?"

"Don't try to dodge responsibility, Leblanc. It won't make you feel better. There isn't one of us without a stronger motive to run the risk than he had." And Stuart sat there silently, thinking.

Mullen felt the obstruction beneath his feet yield and the walls about him slip away quickly, too quickly. He knew it was the puff of air escaping, carrying him with it, and he dug arms and legs frantically against the wall to brake himself. Corpses were supposed to be flung well clear of the ship, but he was no corpse—for the moment.

His feet swung free and threshed. He heard the *clunk* of one magnetic boot against the hull just as the rest of his body puffed out like a tight cork under air pressure. He teetered dangerously at the lip of the hole in the ship—he had changed orientation suddenly and was looking down on it—the took a step backward as its lid came down of itself and fitted smoothly against the hull.

A feeling of unreality overwhelmed him. Surely, it wasn't he standing on the outer surface of a ship. Not Randolph F. Mullen. So few human beings could ever say they had, even those who traveled in space constantly.

He was only gradually aware that he was in pain. Popping out of that hole with one foot clamped to the hull had nearly bent him in two. He tried moving, cautiously, and found his motions to be erratic and almost impossible to control. He *thought* nothing was broken, though the muscles of his left side were badly wrenched.

And then he came to himself and noticed that the wrist lights of his suit were on. It was by their light that he stared into the blackness of the C-chute. He stirred with the nervous thought that from within, the Kloros might see the twin spots of moving light just outside the hull. He flicked the switch upon the suit's mid-section.

Mullen had never imagined that, standing on a ship, he would fail to see its hull. But it was dark, as dark below as above. There were the stars, hard and bright little non-dimensional dots. Nothing more. Nothing more anywhere. Under his feet, not even the stars—*not even his feet.*

He bent back to look at the stars. His head swam. They were moving slowly. Or, rather, they were standing still and the ship was rotating, but he could not tell his eyes that. *They* moved. His eyes followed—down and behind the ship. New stars up and above from the other side. A black horizon. The ship existed only as a region where there were no stars.

No stars? Why, there was one almost at his feet. He nearly reached for it; then he realized that it was only a glittering reflection in the mirroring metal.

They were moving thousands of miles an hour. The stars were. The ship was. He was. But it meant nothing. To his senses, there was only silence and darkness and that slow wheeling of the stars. His eyes followed the wheeling—

And his head in its helmet hit the ship's hull with a soft bell-like ring.

He felt about in panic with his thick, insensitive, spun-silicate gloves. His feet were still firmly magnetized to the hull, that was true, but the rest of his body bent backward at the knees in a right angle. There was no gravity outside the ship. If he bent back, there was nothing to pull the upper part of his body down and tell his joints they were bending. His body stayed as he put it.

He pressed wildly against the hull and his torso shot upward and refused to stop when upright. He fell forward.

He tried more slowly, balancing with both hands against the hull, until he squatted evenly. Then upward. Very slowly. Straight up. Arms out to balance.

He was straight now, aware of his nausea and lightheadedness.

He looked about. My God, where where the steam-tubes? He couldn't see them. They were black on black, nothing on nothing.

Quickly, he turned on the wrist lamps. In space, there were no beams, only elliptical, sharply defined spots of blue steel, winking light back at him. Where they struck a rivet, a shadow was cast, knife-sharp and as black as space, the lighted region illuminated abruptly and without diffusion.

He moved his arms, his body swaying gently in the opposite direction; action and reaction. The vision of a steam-tube with its smooth cylindrical sides sprang at him.

He tried to move toward it. His foot held firmly to the hull. He pulled and it slogged upward, straining against quicksand that eased quickly. Three inches up and it had almost sucked free; six inches up and he thought it would fly away.

He advanced it and let it down, felt it enter the quicksand. When the sole was within two inches of the hull, it snapped down, out of control, hitting the hull ringingly. His spacesuit carried the vibrations, amplifying them in his ears.

He stopped in absolute terror. The dehydrators that dried the atmosphere within his suit could not handle the sudden gush of perspiration that drenched his forehead and armpits.

He waited, then tried lifting his foot again—a bare inch, holding it there by main force and moving it horizontally. Horizontal motion involved no effort at all; it was motion perpendicular to the lines of magnetic force. But he had to keep the foot from snapping down as he did so, and then lower it slowly.

He puffed with the effort. Each step was agony. The tendons of his knees were cracking, and there were knives in his side.

Mullen stopped to let the perspiration dry. It wouldn't do to steam up the inside of his face-plate. He flashed his wrist-lamps, and the steam cylinder was right ahead.

115

The ship had four of them, at ninety degree intervals, thrusting out at an angle from the mid-girdle. They were the "fine adjustment" of the ship's course. The coarse adjustment was the powerfulthrusters back and front which fixed final velocity by their accelerative and decelerative force, and the hyperatomics that took care of the space-swallowing Jumps.

But occasionally the direction of flight had to be adjusted slightly and then the steam-cylinders took over. Singly, they could drive the ship up, down, right, left. By twos, in appropriate ratios of thrust, the ship could be turned in any desired direction.

The device had been unimproved in centuries, being too simple to improve. The atomic pile heated the water content of a closed container into steam, driving it, in less than a second, up to temperatures where it would have broken down into a mixture of hydrogen and oxygen, and then into a mixture of electrons and ions. Perhaps the breakdown actually took place. No one ever bothered testing; it worked, so there was no need to.

At the critical point, a needle valve gave way and the steam thrust madly out in a short but incredible blast. And the ship, inevitably and majestically, moved in the opposite direction, veering about its own center of gravity. When the degrees of turn were sufficient an equal and opposite blast would take place and the turning would be canceled. The ship would be moving at its original velocity, but in a new direction.

Mullen had dragged himself out to the lip of the steam-cylinder. He had a picture of himself—a small speck teetering at the extreme end of a structure thrusting out of an ovoid that was tearing through space at ten thousand miles an hour.

But there was no air-stream to whip him off the hull, and his magnetic soles held him more firmly than he liked.

With lights on, he bent down to peer into the tube and the ship dropped down precipitously as his orientation changed. He reached out to steady himself, but he was not falling. There was no up or down in space except for what his confused mind chose to consider up or down.

The cylinder was just large enough to hold a man, so that it might be entered for repair purposes. His light caught the rungs almost directly opposite his position at the lip. He puffed a sigh of relief with what breath he could muster. Some ships didn't have ladders.

He made his way to it, the ship appearing to slip and twist beneath him as he moved. He lifted an arm over the lip of the tube, feeling for the rung, loosened each foot, and drew himself within.

The knot in his stomach that had been there from the first was a convulsed agony now. If they should choose to manipulate the ship, if the steam should whistle out now—

He would never hear it; never know it. One instant he would be holding a rung, feeling slowly for the next with a groping arm. The next moment he would be alone in space, the ship a dark, dark nothingness lost forever among the stars. There would be, perhaps, a brief glory of swirling ice crystals drifting with him, shining in his wrist light and slowly approaching and rotating about him, attracted by his mass like infinitesimal planets to an absurdly tiny Sun.

He was trickling sweat again, and now he was also conscious of thirst. He put it out of his mind. There would be no drinking until he was out of his suit—if ever.

Up a rung; up another; and another. How many were there? His hand slipped and he stared in disbelief at the glitter that showed under his light.

Ice?

Why not? The steam, incredibly hot as it was, would strike metal that was at nearly absolute zero. In the few split-seconds of thrust, there would not be time for the metal to warm above the freezing point of water. A sheet of ice would condense that would sublime slowly into the vacuum. It was the speed of all that happened that prevented the fusion of the tubes and of the original water-container itself.

His groping hand reached the end. Again the wrist-light. He stared with crawling horror at the steam nozzle, half an inch in diameter. It looked dead, harmless. But it always would, right up to the microsecond before—

Around it was the outer steam lock. It pivoted on a central hub that was springed on the portion toward space, screwed on the part toward the ship. The springs allowed it to give under the first wild thrust of steam pressure before the ship's mighty inertia could be overcome. The steam was bled into the inner chamber, breaking the force of the thrust, leaving the total energy unchanged, but spreading it over time so that the hull itself was in that much less danger of being staved in.

Mullen braced himself firmly against a rung and pressed against the outer lock so that it gave a little. It was stiff, but it didn't have to give much, just enough to catch on the screw. He felt it catch.

He strained against it and turned it, feeling his body twist in the opposite direction. It held tight, the screw taking up the strain as he carefully adjusted the small control switch that allowed the springs to fall free. How well he remembered the books he had read!

He was in the interlock space now, which was large enough to hold a man comfortably, again for convenience in repairs. He could no longer be blown away from the ship. If the steam blast were turned on now, it would merely drive him against the inner lock—hard enough to crush him to a pulp. A quick death he would never feel, at least.

Slowly, he unhooked his spare oxygen cylinder. There was only an inner lock between himself and the control room now. This lock opened outward into space so that the steam blast could only close it tighter, rather than blow it open. And it fitted tightly and smoothly. There was absolutely no way to open it from without.

He lifted himself above the lock, forcing his bent back against the curved inner surface of the interlock area. It made breathing difficult. The spare oxygen cylinder dangled at a queer angle. He held its metal-mesh hose and straightened it, forcing it against the inner lock so that vibration thudded. Again—again—

It would *have* to attract the attention of the Kloros. They would *have* to investigate.

He would have no way of telling when they were about to do so. Ordinarily, they would first let air into the interlock to force the outer lock shut. But now the outer lock was on the central screw, well away from its rim. Air would suck about it ineffectually, dragging out into space.

Mullen kept on thumping. Would the Kloros look at the airgauge, note that it scarcely lifted from zero, or would they take its proper working for granted?

Porter said, "He's been gone and hour and a half."

"I know," said Stuart.

They were all restless, jumpy, but the tension among themselves had disappeared. It was as though all the threads of emotion extended to the hull of the ship.

Porter was bothered. His philosophy of life had always been simple—take care of yourself because no one will take care of you. for you. It upset him to see it shaken.

He said, "Do you suppose they've caught him?"

"If they had, we'd hear about it," replied Stuart, briefly.

Porter felt, with a miserable twinge, that there was little interest on the part of the others in speaking to him. He could understand it; he had not exactly earned their respect. For the moment, a torrent of self-excuse poured through his mind. The others had been frightened, too. A man had a right to be afraid. No one likes to die. At least, he hadn't broken like Aristides Polyorketes. He hadn't wept like Leblanc. He—

But there was Mullen, out there on the hull.

"Listen," he cried, "why did he do it?" They turned to look at him, not understanding, but Porter didn't care. It bothered him to the point where it had to come out. "I want to know why Mullen is risking his life."

"The man," said Windham, "is a patriot—"

"No, none of that!" Porter was almost hysterical. "That little fellow has no emotions at all. He just has reasons and I want to know what those reasons are, because—"

He didn't finish the sentence. Could he say that if those reasons applied to a little middle-aged bookkeeper, they might apply even more forcibly to himself?

Polyorketes said, "He's one brave damn little fellow."

Porter got to his feet. "Listen," he said, "he may be stuck out there. Whatever he's doing, he may not be able to finish it alone. I—I volunteer to go out after him."

He was shaking as he said it and he waited in fear for the sarcastic lash of Stuart's tongue. Stuart was staring at him, probably with surprise, but Porter dared not meet his eyes to make certain.

Stuart said mildly, "Let's give him another half-hour."

Porter looked up, startled. There was no sneer on Stuart's face. It was even friendly. They *all* looked friendly.

He said, "And then—"

"And then all those who do volunteer will draw straws or something equally democratic. Who volunteers, besides Porter?"

They all raised their hands; Stuart did too.

But Porter was happy. He had volunteered first. He was anxious for the half-hour to pass.

It caught Mullen by surprise. The outer lock flew open and the long, thin, snakelike, almost headless neck of a Kloro sucked out, unable to fight the blast of escaping air.

Mullen's cylinder flew away, almost tore free. After one wild moment of frozen panic, he fought for it, dragging it above the air-stream, waiting as long as he dared to let the first fury die down as the air of the control room thinned out, then bringing it down with force.

It caught the sinewy neck squarely, crushing it. Mullen, curled about the lock, almost entirely protected from the stream, raised the cylinder again and plunging it down again, striking the head,

119

mashing the staring eyes to liquid ruin. In the near-vacuum, green blood was pumping out of what was left of the neck.

Mullen dared not vomit, but he wanted to.

With eyes averted, he backed away, caught the outer lock with one hand and imparted a whirl. For several seconds, it maintained that whirl. At the end of the screw, the springs engaged automatically and pulled it shut. What was left of the atmosphere tightened it and the laboring pumps could now begin to fill the control room once again.

Mullen crawled over the mangled Kloro and into the room. It was empty.

He had barely time to notice that when he found himself on his knees. He rose with difficulty. The transition from non-gravity to gravity had taken him entirely by surprise. It was Klorian gravity, too, which meant that with this suit, he carried a fifty percent overload for his small frame. At least, though, his heavy metal clogs no longer clung so exasperatingly to the metal underneath. Within the ship, floors and walls were of cork-covered aluminium alloy.

He circled slowly. The neckless Kloro had collapsed and lay with only an occasional twitch to show it had once been a living organism. He stepped over it, distastefully, and drew the steam-tube lock shut.

The room had a depressing bilious cast and the lights shone yellow-green. It was the Kloro atmosphere, of course.

Mullen felt a twinge of surprise and reluctant admiration. The Kloros obviously had some way of treating materials so that they were impervious to the oxidizing effect of chlorine. Even the map of Earth on the wall, printed on glossy plastic-backed paper, seemed fresh and untouched. He approached, drawn by the familiar outlines of the continents—

There was a flash of motion caught in the corner of his eyes. As quickly as he could in his heavy suit, he turned, then screamed. The Kloro he had thought dead was rising to its feet.

Its neck hung limp, an oozing mass of tissue mash, but its arms reached out blindly, and the tentacles about its chest vibrated rapidly like innumerable snakes' tongues.

It was blind, of course. The destruction of its neck-stalk had deprived it of all sensory equipment, and partial asphyxiation had disorganized it. But the brain remained whole and safe in the abdomen. It still lived.

Mullen backed away. He circled, trying clumsily and unsuccessfully to tiptoe, though he knew that what was left of the

120

Kloro was also deaf. It blundered on its way, struck a wall, felt to the base and began sidling along it.

Mullen cast about desperately for a weapon, found nothing. There was the Kloro's holster, but he dared not reach for it. Why hadn't he snatched it at the very first? Fool!

The door to the control room opened. It made almost no noise. Mullen turned quivering.

The other Kloro entered, unharmed, entire. It stood in the doorway for a moment, chest-tendrils stiff and unmoving; its neck-stalk stretched forward; its horrible eyes flickering first at him and then at its nearly dead comrade.

And then its hand moved quickly to its side.

Mullen, without awareness, moved as quickly in pure reflex. He stretched out the hose of the spare oxygen-cylinder, which, since entering the control room, he had replaced in its suit-clamp, and cracked the valve. He didn't bother reducing the pressure. He let it gush out unchecked so that he nearly staggered under the backward push.

He could *see* the oxygen stream. It was a pale puff, billowing out amid the chlorine-green. It caught the Kloro with one hand on the weapon's holster.

The Kloro threw its hands up. The little beak on its head-nodule opened alarmingly but noiselessly. It staggered and fell, writhed for a moment, then lay still. Mullen approached and played the oxygen-stream upon its body as though he were extinguishing a fire. And then he raised his heavy foot and brought it down upon the center of the neck-stalk and crushed it on the floor.

He turned to the first. It was sprawled, rigid.

The whole room was pale with oxygen, enough to kill whole legions of Kloros, and his cylinder was empty.

Mullen stepped over the dead Kloro, out of the control room and along the main corridor toward the prisoners' room.

Reaction had set in. He was whimpering in blind, incoherent fright.

Stuart was tired. False hands and all, he was at the controls of a ship once again. Two light cruisers of Earth were on the way. For better than twenty-four hours he had handled the controls virtually alone. He had discarded the chlorinating equipment, rerigged the old atmospherics, located the ship's position in space, tried to plot a course, and sent out carefully guarded signals—which had worked.

So when the door of the control room opened, he was a little annoyed. He was too tired to play conversational handball. Then he turned, and it was Mullen stepping inside.

Stuart said, "For God's sake, get back into bed, Mullen!"

Mullen said, "I'm tired of sleeping even though I never thought I would be a while ago."

"How do you feel?"

"I'm stiff all over. Especially my side." He grimaced and stared involuntarily around.

"Don't look for the Kloros," Stuart said. "We dumped the poor devils." He shook his head. "I was sorry for them. To themselves *they're* the human beings, you know, and *we're* the aliens. Not that I'd rather they'd killed you, you understand."

"I understand."

Stuart turned a sidelong glance upon the little man who sat looking at the map of Earth and went on, "I owe you a particular and personal apology, Mullen. I didn't think much of you."

"It was your privilege," said Mullen in his dry voice. There was no feeling in it.

"No, it wasn't. It is no one's privilege to despise another. It is only a hard-won right after long experience."

"Have you been thinking about this?"

"Yes, all day. Maybe I can't explain. It's these hands." He held them up before him, spread out. "It was hard knowing that other people had hands of their own. I had to hate them for it. I always had to do my best to investigate and belittle their motives, point up their deficiencies, expose their stupidities. I had to do anything that would prove to myself that they weren't worth envying."

Mullen moved restlessly. "This explanation is not necessary."

"It is. It is!" Stuart felt his thoughts intently, strained to put them into words. "For years I've abandoned hope of finding any decency in human beings. Then you climbed into the C-chute."

"You had better understand," said Mullen, "that I was motivated by practical and selfish considerations. I will not have you present me to myself as a hero."

"I wasn't intending to. I know that you would do nothing without a reason. It was what your action did to the rest of us. It turned a collection of phonies and fools into decent people. And not by magic either. They were decent all along. It was just that they needed something to live up to and you supplied it. And— I'm one of them. I'll have to live up to you, too. For the rest of my life, probably."

Mullen turned away uncomfortably. His hand straightened his

122

sleeves, which were not in the least twisted. His finger rested on the map.

He said, "I was born in Richmond, Virginia, you know. Here it is. I'll be going there first. Where were you born?"

"Toronto." said Stuart.

"That's right here. Not very far apart on the map, is it?"

Stuart said, "Would you tell me something?"

"If I can."

"Just why *did* you go out there?"

Mullen's precise mouth pursed. He said, dryly, "Wouldn't my rather prosaic reason ruin the inspirational effect?"

"Call it intellectual curiosity. Each of the rest of us had such obvious motives. Porter was scared to death of being interned; Leblanc wanted to get back to his sweetheart; Polyorketes wanted to kill Kloros; and Windham was a patriot according to his lights. As for me, I thought of myself as a noble idealist. I'm afraid. Yet in none of us was the motivation strong enough to get us into a spacesuit and out the C-chute. Then what made *you* do it, *you*, of all people?"

"Why the phrase, 'of all people'?"

"Don't be offended, but you seem devoid of all emotion."

"Do I?" Mullen's voice did not change. It remained precise and soft, yet somehow a tightness had entered it. "That's only training, Mr. Stuart, and self-discipline; not nature. A small man can have no respectable emotions. Is there anything more ridiculous than a man like myself in a state of rage? I'm five feet and one-half inch tall, and one hundred and two pounds in weight, if you care for exact figures. I insist on the half inch and the two pounds.

"Can I be dignified? Proud? Draw myself to my full height without inducing laughter? Where can I meet a woman who will not dismiss me instantly with a giggle? Naturally, I've had to learn to dispense with external display of emotion.

"*You* talk about deformities. No one would notice your hands or know they were different, if you weren't so eager to tell people all about it the instant you meet them. Do you think that the eight inches of height I do not have can be hidden? That is not the first and, in most cases, the only thing about me that a person will notice?"

Stuart was ashamed. He had invaded a privacy he ought not have. He said, "I'm sorry."

"Why?"

"I should not have forced you to speak of this. I should have seen for myself that you—that you—"

123

"That I what? Tried to prove myself? Tried to show that while I might be small in body, I held within it a giant's heart?"

"I would not have put it mockingly."

"Why not? It's a foolish idea, and nothing like it is the reason I did what I did. What would I have accomplished if that's what was in my mind? Will they take me to Earth now and put me up before the television cameras—pitching them low, of course, to catch my face, or standing me on a chair—and pin medals on me?"

"They are quite likely to do exactly that."

"And what good would it do me? They would say, 'Gee, and he's such a little guy.' And afterward, what? Shall I tell each man I meet, 'You know, I'm the fellow they decorated for incredible valor last month?' How may medals, Mr. Stuart, do you suppose it would take to put eight inches and sixty pounds on me?"

Stuart said, "Put that away, I see your point."

Mullen was speaking a trifle more quickly now; a controlled heat had entered his words, warming them to just a tepid room temperature. "There *were* days when I thought I would show them, the mysterious 'them' that includes all the world. I was going to leave Earth and carve out worlds for myself. I would be a new and even smaller Napoleon. So I left Earth and went to Arcturus. And what could I do on Arcturus that I could not have done on Earth? Nothing. I balance books. So I am past the vanity, Mr. Stuart, of trying to stand on tiptoe."

"Then why *did* you do it?"

"I left Earth when I was twenty-eight and came to the Arcturian System. I've been there ever since. This trip was to be my first vacation, my first visit back to Earth in all that time. I was going to stay on Earth for six months. The Kloros instead captured us and would have kept us interned indefinitely. But I couldn't—I *couldn't* let them stop me from traveling to Earth. No matter what the risk, I had to prevent their interference. It wasn't love of woman, or fear, or hate, or idealism of any sort. It was stronger than any of those."

He stopped, and stretched out a hand as though to caress the map on the wall.

"Mr. Stuart," Mullen asked quietly, "haven't you ever been homesick?"

PIRATES OF THE ASTEROIDS

by Isaac Asimov

An ever-increasing mystery lures David Starr into a perilous journey across a galaxy to destroy a marauding band of space privateers. Twenty-five years ago these vermin had killed his parents. All his life he had waited for the moment of vengeance. Now, that moment was very near.

THE NEW ENGLISH LIBRARY

SPACE RANGER
by Isaac Asimov

Space Ranger is a story of a cunning and brutal
conspiracy by aliens to cripple the economy of Earth.

Poisoning from Martian colony and danger of mass
panic present a threat to the very fabric of Earth's
government.

The dark wings of Death brush low across our planet.
Only the multi-faceted talents of Isaac Asimov could
have produced this star-toppling series of David Starr –
a series that will open new vistas of pleasure for his
legion of admirers.

THE NEW ENGLISH LIBRARY

NEL BESTSELLERS

Crime

T013 332	CLOUDS OF WITNESS	*Dorothy L. Sayers* 40p
T016 307	THE UNPLEASANTNESS AT THE BELLONA CLUB	
		Dorothy L. Sayers 40p
T021 548	GAUDY NIGHT	*Dorothy L. Sayers* 40p
T026 698	THE NINE TAILORS	*Dorothy L. Sayers* 40p
T026 671	FIVE RED HERRINGS	*Dorothy L. Sayers* 50p
T015 556	MURDER MUST ADVERTISE	*Dorothy L. Sayers* 40p

Fiction

T018 520	HATTER'S CASTLE	*A. J. Cronin* 75p
T013 944	CRUSADER'S TOMB	*A. J. Cronin* 60p
T013 936	THE JUDAS TREE	*A. J. Cronin* 50p
T015 386	THE NORTHERN LIGHT	*A. J. Cronin* 50p
T026 213	THE CITADEL	*A. J. Cronin* 80p
T027 112	BEYOND THIS PLACE	*A. J. Cronin* 60p
T016 609	KEYS OF THE KINGDOM	*A. J. Cronin* 60p
T027 201	THE STARS LOOK DOWN	*A. J. Cronin* 90p
T018 539	A SONG OF SIXPENCE	*A. J. Cronin* 50p
T001 288	THE TROUBLE WITH LAZY ETHEL	*Ernest K. Gann* 30p
T003 922	IN THE COMPANY OF EAGLES	*Ernest K. Gann* 30p
T023 001	WILDERNESS BOY	*Stephen Harper* 35p
T017 524	MAGGIE D	*Adam Kennedy* 60p
T022 390	A HERO OF OUR TIME	*Mikhail Lermontov* 45p
T025 691	SIR, YOU BASTARD	*G. F. Newman* 40p
T022 536	THE HARRAD EXPERIMENT	*Robert H. Rimmer* 50p
T022 994	THE DREAM MERCHANTS	*Harold Robbins* 95p
T023 303	THE PIRATE	*Harold Robbins* 95p
T022 968	THE CARPETBAGGERS	*Harold Robbins* £1·00
T016 560	WHERE LOVE HAS GONE	*Harold Robbins* 75p
T023 958	THE ADVENTURERS	*Harold Robbins* £1·00
T025 241	THE INHERITORS	*Harold Robbins* 90p
T025 276	STILETTO	*Harold Robbins* 50p
T025 268	NEVER LEAVE ME	*Harold Robbins* 50p
T025 292	NEVER LOVE A STRANGER	*Harold Robbins* 90p
T022 226	A STONE FOR DANNY FISHER	*Harold Robbins* 80p
T025 284	79 PARK AVENUE	*Harold Robbins* 75p
T025 187	THE BETSY	*Harold Robbins* 80p
T020 894	RICH MAN, POOR MAN	*Irwin Shaw* 90p

Historical

T022 196	KNIGHT WITH ARMOUR	*Alfred Duggan* 50p
T022 250	THE LADY FOR RANSOM	*Alfred Duggan* 50p
T015 297	COUNT BOHEMOND	*Alfred Duggan* 50p
T017 958	FOUNDING FATHERS	*Alfred Duggan* 50p
T017 753	WINTER QUARTERS	*Alfred Duggan* 50p
T021 297	FAMILY FAVOURITES	*Alfred Duggan* 50p
T022 625	LEOPARDS AND LILIES	*Alfred Duggan* 60p
T019 624	THE LITTLE EMPERORS	*Alfred Duggan* 50p
T020 126	THREE'S COMPANY	*Alfred Duggan* 50p
T021 300	FOX 10: BOARDERS AWAY	*Adam Hardy* 35p

Science Fiction

T016 900	STRANGER IN A STRANGE LAND	*Robert Heinlein* 75p
T020 797	STAR BEAST	*Robert Heinlein* 35p
T017 451	I WILL FEAR NO EVIL	*Robert Heinlein* 80p
T026 817	THE HEAVEN MAKERS	*Frank Herbert* 35p
T027 279	DUNE	*Frank Herbert* 90p
T022 854	DUNE MESSIAH	*Frank Herbert* 60p
T023 974	THE GREEN BRAIN	*Frank Herbert* 35p
T012 859	QUEST FOR THE FUTURE	*A. E. Van Vogt* 35p
T015 270	THE WEAPON MAKERS	*A. E. Van Vogt* 30p
T023 265	EMPIRE OF THE ATOM	*A. E. Van Vogt* 40p
T017 354	THE FAR-OUT WORLDS OF A. E. VAN VOGT	*A. E. Van Vogt* 40p

War

T027 066	COLDITZ: THE GERMAN STORY	Reinhold Eggers	50p
T009 890	THE K BOATS	Don Everett	30p
T020 854	THE GOOD SHEPHERD	C. S. Forester	35p
T012 999	P.Q. 17 – CONVOY TO HELL	Lund & Ludlam	30p
T026 299	TRAWLERS GO TO WAR	Lund & Ludlam	50p
T010 872	BLACK SATURDAY	Alexander McKee	30p
T020 495	ILLUSTRIOUS	Kenneth Poolman	40p
T018 032	ARK ROYAL	Kenneth Poolman	40p
T027 198	THE GREEN BERET	Hilary St George Saunders	50p
T027 171	THE RED BERET	Hilary St George Saunders	50p

Western

T016 994	EDGE NO 1: THE LONER	George Gilman	30p
T024 040	EDGE NO 2: TEN THOUSAND DOLLARS AMERICAN		
		George Gilman	35p
T024 075	EDGE NO 3: APACHE DEATH	George Gilman	35p
T024 032	EDGE NO 4: KILLER'S BREED	George Gilman	35p
T023 990	EDGE NO 5: BLOOD ON SILVER	George Gilman	35p
T020 002	EDGE NO 14: THE BIG GOLD	George Gilman	30p

General

T017 400	CHOPPER	Peter Cave	30p
T022 838	MAMA	Peter Cave	35p
T021 009	SEX MANNERS FOR MEN	Robert Chartham	35p
T019 403	SEX MANNERS FOR ADVANCED LOVERS	Robert Chartham	30p
T023 206	THE BOOK OF LOVE	Dr David Delvin	90p
P002 368	AN ABZ OF LOVE	Inge & Stan Hegeler	75p
P011 402	A HAPPIER SEX LIFE	Dr Sha Kokken	70p
W24 79	AN ODOUR OF SANCTITY	Frank Yerby	50p
W28 24	THE FOXES OF HARROW	Frank Yerby	50p

Mad

S006 086	MADVERTISING	40p
S006 292	MORE SNAPPY ANSWERS TO STUPID QUESTIONS	40p
S006 425	VOODOO MAD	40p
S006 293	MAD POWER	40p
S006 291	HOPPING MAD	40p

··

NEL P.O. BOX 11, FALMOUTH, CORNWALL

For U.K. & Eire: customers should include to cover postage, 15p for the first book plus 5p per copy for each additional book ordered, up to a maximum charge of 50p.

For Overseas customers & B.F.P.O.: customers should include to cover postage, 20p for the first book and 10p per copy for each additional book.

Name ....

Address..

....

Title ....
(MAY)